Brother Harry
and
The Hobo

by LaJoyce Martin

Brother Harry and The Hobo

by LaJoyce Martin

©Copyright 1998 Word Aflame Press
Hazelwood, MO 63042-2299

Cover Design by Paul Povolni
Cover Art by Bob Watkins

All Scripture quotations in this book are from the King James Version of the Bible unless otherwise identified.

Printed in United States of America.

Printed by

WORD AFLAME®PRESS
8855 DUNN ROAD
HAZELWOOD, MO 63042-2299

Library of Congress Cataloging-in-Publication Data

Martin, LaJoyce, 1937–
     Brother Harry and the hobo / by LaJoyce Martin.
       p.   cm.
     ISBN 1-56722-228-5
     I. Title.
PS3563.A72486B78   1999
813' .54—dc21
                                        98-52729
                                          CIP

Brother Harry
and
The Hobo

Other Books by LaJoyce Martin:

The Harris Family Saga:
To Love a Bent-Winged Angel
Love's Mended Wings
Love's Golden Wings
When Love Filled the Gap
To Love a Runaway
A Single Worry
Two Scars Against One
The Fiddler's Song
The Artist's Quest

Pioneer Romance:
The Wooden Heart
Heart-Shaped Pieces
Light in the Evening Time
To Strike a Match
Love's Velvet Chains
Destiny's Winding Road
Mister B's Land

Historical Romance:
So Swift the Storm
So Long the Night

Historical Novel:
Thread's End

Western:
The Other Side of Jordan
To Even the Score

Path of Promise:
The Broken Bow
Ordered Steps

Children's Short Stories:
Batteries for My Flashlight

Nonfiction:
Mother Eve's Garden Club
Heroes, Sheroes, and a Few Zeroes
I'm Coming Apart, Lord!
Alpha-Toons
Coriander Seed and Honey

Contents

CHAPTER 1

Troubles

Brother Harry's troubles came in threes.

Three women.

Three hoodlums.

And a salary of three dollars a week. That is, if there was enough in the treasury for that stipend.

At forty-three years of age, he pastored the only church in Roberts County. The county boasted but one town, and the town but one dusty street. On this dusty street squatted Brother Harry's small clapboard church.

He had been the parson for three months, and he saw that he had his work cut out for him. Outnumbered in a coterie of fluttering, flattering females, he found himself the recipient of knitted bed socks, baked goods and lavender-scented notes.

"May the grace of heaven help me!" he muttered. "What does a single man do with the lady admirers?"

The chief request of the sparse congregation had been that he visit them regularly. Three times a week? How could he have known when he accepted the position that three of these members were of the fairer sex with amorous intentions?

Nor had he taken into consideration the lawlessness of such an isolated hamlet, dubbed by the locals as a "fuel stop" because the train halted for water when it came through with its load of coal, cattle, and hoboes. He'd already run head-on into three ruffians bent on mischief with himself as their pigeon. One of them was the sheriff's son.

He had also crossed paths with the hoboes, but they were harmless drifters cursed with the unfortunate leaven of restlessness in their clay. He didn't mind sharing his meals with them, ignoring their dirt and their odor, hoping to wield some spiritual influence. The breath of life in a being was the only prerequisite for his concern.

The offering had fallen in arrears a couple of times, but for the most part he had gotten the money he was promised. A ten-percent "tithe for the Lord" went back to the church, leaving only $2.70. Half of that made the payment on his Model T, a must for a minister with the distance that fell his lot to cover. Buying the car had taken all of his cash reserve, and it ate into two years of his future wages in the form of monthly installments. Brother Harry was a man who would pay his debts before he bought necessities.

The kitchen clock struck seven. Brother Harry pushed back the patched curtain and saw that the hills to the north were up to their knees in mist. An anemic sun seemed in no hurry to chase the fog away. He jumped from his bed and walked the three steps to the washbasin, where he picked up his granddad's straight razor, stropped it a few times, lathered his chin with the soap in the mug, and removed all traces of stubble with a dozen swift strokes. Then he got dressed, matching his sleeve garters to his galluses.

His habit was to have a time of private devotion before he left the parsonage. He sat down in a tall cane-bottomed chair, his feet searching for space, and picked up his Bible. It fell open to Proverbs, to a very frightening passage of Scripture: *It is better to dwell in a corner of the housetop, than with a brawling woman in a wide house.* He closed the Book at once and jerked his hands away. Was God trying to tell him something?

Certainly, his dwelling was no bigger than the corner of an attic. The one-room cottage, filled to overflowing with his deceased mother's furniture, allowed no leeway to move about. The bed nudged the chiffonier, which bumped the table that crowded the washstand. An old trunk played piggyback for a wooden quilt box that bore the burden of a violin case on its own lid. He wished for a wider house, but not at the expense of a brawling woman!

Brother Harry had given little thought to marriage; life hadn't afforded him that opportunity. His father died when he was a tad of a boy, heaping upon his young shoulders a man's responsibility. He had a mother and two younger sisters to care for.

Both of the girls wed in their early teens, and it might be supposed that one or the other would care for her mother. But no. The job was left to Brother Harry, a patient soul who bore his load bravely and without complaint.

Mother Porter had been dead a year now. Harry's sisters—worldly girls they were—took the pretty quilts, the crocheted doilies, the carnival glass dishes, and the sterling silver, but they didn't want the "tacky, worn-out furniture." Harry made no objection to what they took or left behind, bringing the fragments along with him to Roberts County. With food and raiment, the Lord said, be content.

Harry's mother knew for some time that she was going to cross Jordan. She was at peace with her Maker, and the prospect of departing this world bothered her not at all. What did bother her was that her passing would leave Harry all alone. "After I am gone, you must find you a good wife, my Harry," she said.

"But how shall I know how to choose a good wife?" Harry asked. "They all look alike to me."

"Ah, my son, your own wisdom is not sufficient for the choice. You can be fooled," she warned. "But God shall direct your heart to a woman of reason, courage, and grace. The first plus the second equals the third."

Harry had never been adept with equations. Mixing English in the formula would make finding the solution more difficult. He tried to make sense of what his mother said but only became more confused.

Before his mother's passing, Harry had preached a bit at brush arbor services and open-air revivals, and she had been proud of him. She thought him the world's best orator. "But someday you will be a parson with a church of your own," she prophesied, "and then you will need a helpmate."

The time had come. But just now he thought of every reason that he should not have a helpmate. The parsonage was too small for one person, let alone two. Three dollars a week, split midways by an outstanding car debt, would not feed another mouth. And of the three women coveting him, he didn't have a clue as to which one to pick.

Exactly how he came to take the Roberts County church was still murky in Brother Harry's mind. It had been without a pastor for several months, the building abandoned and left to its own idea of decay. An old church it was, set in its ways, satisfied to drift along, singing the old hymns with no patience for upgrading. Now that he had been here a few weeks, he decided that no one else *wanted* the church; he'd had no competition.

It was rumored that the hooligans worried the last preacher away. Already they had put water in his gas tank, and he'd had to siphon it out; they had pelted his church with hens' eggs; and they had upturned his outhouse. Nothing really serious, but who was to say what they might do next?

On his iron cook stove, Brother Harry made some cornmeal mush for breakfast. That was a chore he would be glad to turn over to a woman: cooking. The substances he wanted smooth had lumps, and those he wanted with lumps turned to liquid. It was a frustrating task.

A note on the table reminded him to water his tomato plants. He had written it to himself. Humoring a garden was another new experience for Harry. In a plot no larger than an outsized bedspread, he seeded a few radishes and set out half a dozen tomato plants, some peppers, and cucumbers—vegetables that would require no cooking. He was discovering a funny thing about gardening: it grew on you. You started out hating it, but once you worked the aches out of your back, you almost liked it. It was a pleasant diversion that gave a quiet sense of achievement. He hastened out the back door and drew water from the pump to encourage the vines that were bravely trying to pull themselves from the drooping stage of transplant.

In the house again, he snatched his list, aware that he was getting a later than usual start on his rounds. That would mean less time for each visit. Who would he short-change today?

He checked the names. *Fiona Hawksbury*. She was one of "the three." Dark-haired, blue-eyed, and with enough energy for three people. As women went, he sup-posed, Fiona was exceedingly attractive. Why she had never married was a puzzle. She must be on the dark side of thirty. Thirty-six or thirty-seven, probably. She had a penchant for asking the most devastating questions with an air of complete innocence. There was one thing that went unquestioned: she wouldn't let him redeem his lost time at her expense. She would usurp the whole hour and more if he would allow.

Pick up shirts. That notation was on his list, too. Ironing was outside the realm of his capabilities. He pressed more wrinkles in than he pressed out. Therefore, he was obliged to hire his collars done, which took anoth-er dollar a month from his scant purse.

Widow Allison did the laundering of his shirts, and she was one of "the three" as well. Harry wasn't versed on romance, but he had been informed by the town gossip that the widow was interested in him. "Watch that woman!" blazed a note left in the seat of his coupe and anchored with a rock. "The quiet ones are the dangerous ones."

The widow was an insignificant little woman: forty-fiveish, dumpy, soft-voiced, and gentle-eyed. A comfortable pudding, cheerful and no stranger to work was Harry's appraisal when he first came to Roberts County. And he'd had no reason to revise his estimate.

His stop by the widow's place would be fleeting. He would knock. She would hand out the shirts on wooden hangers. He would give her the quarter and tell her he would bring more ironing next Monday. A business call, that's all.

He planned a noontime pause by the rail tank to see if any hoboes swung off the boxcars today. He used any ruse to witness, and these poor wanderers needed the gospel. Their souls were as important as the next.

Harry drew himself a little map so as not to occasion an extra inch of travel. He was running dangerously low on funds this month, and his budget for gasoline had already been overextended. He hurried to his vehicle.

The hoodlums had let the air out of his tires.

CHAPTER 2

Party Line

Everybody knew everything there was to know about everybody else in town because everyone was on the same party line. Everyone, that is, except Brother Harry. He had no telephone and no hankering for one. The three women would drive him insane if he had a talking box!

If one wanted to listen in on a conversation, all one had to do was pick up the receiver and favor it with an eager ear. And there was an abundance of eager ears in this cloistered and curiosity-bitten community. A scent of scandal was their favorite perfume. The village had no need for a newspaper; its news would be stale by the time the ink was dry.

Just now the third female on the parson's trouble list, an old maid with her mind congealed in a certainty that God had sent Brother Harry to Roberts County for her matrimonial benefit, listened to the chatter between Fiona Hawksbury and Widow Allison with a smug smile. *Talk all you wish. Argue all you wish. Plan all you wish.*

Brother Harry is mine. Our lives are linked by fate.

The more Maybelle Davis heard, the broader her grin. Fiona was pouring her venom on the poor widow. Jealousy scorched the phone line. "I know that you have your calf eyes turned on the new parson, Grace Allison, but you might as well moon another direction. You haven't a chance. Why, Brother Harry wouldn't give you an alderman's glance!"

"I'm not mooning at anybody, Fiona."

"Ho. Tell me another shaggy dog story! I've watched you sit there on the bench at church and drool when you should be tending to those kids of yours or, at the least, thinking about God."

"It is unfortunate that you waste your time watching me, dear. There are certainly more interesting personalities than I. You might watch Deacon Shone's wife or Mrs. Turner or—"

"Then, Mrs. Allison, if you haven't ideas, let this serve as a warning not to invent any. You've had your chance at wedded bliss, while some of the rest of us are waiting in line. You are old enough to be the parson's mother."

"He is only a year and five months younger than I."

"How should you know the parson's age, Grace?"

"I—"

"And his birth date? Ha! I caught you, didn't I?"

"Deacon Shone told all of us Brother Harry's age before he came, remember? He is forty-three. And he shares a birthday with John-John, my youngest. He told my son, and my son told me. In fact, he said that he and John-John would celebrate their birthdays together."

"Well, John can forget that! I will see that Brother Harry has a proper birthday dinner, Grace. With crystal and linen. I hope that John won't be too disappointed."

"As you will, Fiona, and blessings on you."

It appeared that the widow was ready to ring off, but Fiona wasn't through. "Anyhow, there's some rule in the Bible that instructs those in God's service to marry a woman who has never been wed before."

"Oh?"

"It's there in black and white."

"In the old law, I believe."

"Wherever. It is in the Bible, and Brother Harry is a Bible-abiding man. I will ask him to look that up for me just to be sure."

"Never mind, Fiona."

"Oh, you won't talk me out of it, Grace. I plan to bring it to the parson's attention right away."

"If I am too old for the parson, dear, don't you think you are a bit young?"

"No. Being a parson's wife takes radiant health and energy. I have both. There's something you might as well know, Gracie. The first time I laid eyes on Brother Harry, I knew he was the man with whom I wanted to spend the rest of my life. Why, I've waited for a man of the cloth since I was a lass in pinafores. I have saved my virtue— well, almost—for such a time as this. I feel the blessed bonding taking place already. Brother Harry loves Frazzles."

"Who?"

"Frazzles. My precious pooch."

"Look, Fiona, I hate to ring off so soon, but I have a shirt to iron this morning."

"For one of the boys?"

"No. For the parson."

During the moment of strained silence, metered breathing could be heard along the line, and once a suppressed hiccup came through clearly. Then Fiona emitted a hard laugh. "Ah, it is good, Grace, that our beloved parson considers you nothing more than a washerwoman. Caress his shirts all you please. Hug them. Kiss them, for that is as close as you will get to the man I plan to marry. Good day."

The line went dead, and clicks echoed down the wire from one end to the other. The supper table talk would be lively tonight, retelling the garnered hearsay.

Maybelle laughed outright. She would simply bide her time. The drama that included her reminded her of Goldilocks and the three bears. Grace Allison was too old for the parson, and Fiona Hawksbury was too young. Grace was too poor, and Fiona too rich. Grace was too fat, and Fiona too thin. Grace had beloved children, and Fiona had a precious dog. Grace . . . Fiona . . . She, Maybelle Davis, was just right. She had nothing but time and affection for a man who needed no other trappings to make him happy. Besides, she could play the piano. She would win.

It was late when Brother Harry arrived at Fiona's imposing house. He'd had to pump air into all four tires plus the spare, which he found hidden under the front stoop. The sheriff had delayed him for a chat, as well as the postman. No hoboes disembarked today, though, a boon to his flagging schedule.

A tedious and frustrating day it had been. His plans had met with disaster, his hopes with sabotage. The vanilla flavoring he had daubed under his arms had lost its power, but there was only one stop after Fiona's, thank heaven. His face was flushed with rushing when he got to her place.

"Oh, Brother Harry," babbled Fiona as a ball of white fur squeezed past her, yapping and nipping at the man's ankles. (How he detested that spoiled animal!) "Now, Frazzles, do behave," she scolded. "Brother Harry, that dog worships you! Why, he loves you better than any man who has ever called on me. And there have been oodles of them. That's a good sign, don't you think?"

"That there have been lots of—?"

"Oh, no, no! That my Frazzles is so fond of you."

He wondered what he should say, and finding nothing, he said nothing. While her sycophancy should have lifted his spirits, it lowered them instead. What should he care for the affection of a woman's dog?

Fiona's voice droned on and on like a bee buzzing about the window on a drowsy midsummer day. Then—suddenly—the buzzing stopped. An awkward silence ensued. Harry came back to the present with a start. He suspected that Fiona had asked one of those devastating questions.

"Isn't that in the Bible, sir?"

Harry blinked. Belatedly, he reined in his runaway thoughts. "I'm sorry, I was thinking about the—the dog. What was the question?"

"I said, isn't there a verse in the Bible that directs the ethics of a minister's marriage?"

"I—I—" Something like a bird in Harry's head beat its wings faster and faster against the walls of his tired brain. Frazzles lunged at his leg with sadistic intensity, but Fiona jerked the dog's leash.

"I was sure that there was such a Scripture," she said,

pursing her lips and making her eyes wide with girlish appeal. "It seems I read it once."

"I don't recall—"

"The preachers were only to marry virgins, weren't they?"

"Oh, yes, you must be referring to the high priests who served in the Tabernacle of Moses. The law said they were to wed someone who had never been married."

"That's what I told Grace Allison, and she pretended she had never heard of that particular text. Of course, that would rule her out of marrying a reverend. And I reminded her of it."

"It is a matter of how one interprets an issue, I presume. It seems—"

"Anyhow, she has three children."

"Very lovely and well-mannered children they are," he said, glancing about at the long and clearly defined shadows that slanted across the yard. "I have a quick errand to run before dark, Miss Hawksbury, if you will excuse me."

The sounds of the Model T, chugging away in the dim distance, could still be heard when Fiona snatched up the phone. "Operator," she demanded, "give me 292-J." There was a very slight delay on the part of the operator. "And hurry!" thundered Fiona.

Grace answered her ring as earpieces lifted all along the way to get their part of the day's gabble. "Hello?"

"Grace," Fiona said without preamble, "about that verse. It *is* in the Bible. I told you so."

"What verse, Fiona?"

"The one about—"

"Just a minute, Fiona. The parson is here to pick up

his shirts. Hang on for a second, and I'll be back." She dropped the apparatus and went for Brother Harry's laundry.

Fiona could hear them talking, but the conversation was maddeningly incomprehensible. The voices drifted farther and farther away until they were no longer in range of the listeners. Then a screen door slammed, and there was a long stretch of dead air.

The truth is that the parson took his immediate leave, but Grace answered the beck of young John to view a hatch of baby birds in a tree nest. So caught up was Grace with the wonder of nature that she completely forgot about the dangling receiver, Fiona's call, or the verse. She sat in the porch swing with her children watching God push the moon up and make a beautiful night.

An hour later, when the stars made dot-to-dots in the heavens, she went inside to light the coal oil lamps. With an embarrassed gasp, she caught up the telephone, but Fiona had long since hung up.

The eavesdroppers assumed that Grace Allison had spent the entire time in the fellowship of the parson. Among them was the town gossip.

CHAPTER 3

Boze

The hobo liked the Roberts County village. He liked its friendly ambience, its isolation, and its mild climate. He enjoyed the nuances in the weather of this southwestern land. The sky could seem clear one day, yet sometime during the night—without rain or cloud—a mysterious desert wind would sweep the heavens so that the following morning brought an atmosphere purer than if the area had been rinsed by storm and rain.

He found less prejudice here than in other places he had been. There was a curious absence of time and hurry, and the yesterdays counted for little. Besides, he liked to fish in Red Deer Creek.

His first streak of good fortune was to hit it off with the sheriff's son, Dub. Dub called him Boze, which, agreed the hobo, was as good a name as any. He had been called worse, he laughed.

"I like for people to suit their names," Dub said. "Boze fits you."

Boze appeared to be about sixty, give or take a few

years, and he walked with a decided hobble. His dirty white hair sprouted through a tattered felt hat that had suffered a blowout. He wore ragged overalls and over-sized shoes and had a plump midsection.

Along with a scar on his left cheek, always more grimy than the area around it, he had a bandaged eye. The patch on his right eye made him look more like a pirate than a hobo. Maybe that's why the hoodlums grav-itated to him. He appealed to their rebel spirits, telling wondrous stories of faraway places.

Dub, the eighteen-year-old ringleader of the gang-sters, was an enigma to the hobo. Every ounce of him was solid muscle, his chest thick. Although as hard as flint on the outside, he had a jelly-soft core. His actions often betrayed his mouth. A battle raged within him; Boze could see it in the boy's eyes even when he spoke in his most arrogant, slap-in-the-face manner. *It is almost as if he is two people rolled into one piecrust*, thought the hobo.

Dub introduced Boze to the other two members of the gang, both considerably younger than their kingpin. Their names were Nick and Harlo. These were not bad guys, Boze determined. They were bored guys. Adolescence was the age of herd instinct. To be different from one's peers could mean despair. Channeled, their mischief might actually prove beneficial to the little town in which they lived. They needed a leader, and who was more capa-ble than he was?

It wasn't long before Boze had the boys eating out of his hand, and he knew it. He told them about a club he had initiated in his own pre-manhood days; he suggested that the four of them form a partnership. One would not do anything without the agreement of the others. The majority would rule. Three could always outvote one. Their meeting place would be in a cave near Red Deer Creek.

Right away, Boze learned that the villains had no use for the preacher. They called him "Preach." "We ran the last one off," Harlo boasted. "Anybody that works one day a week and begs for other people's money with an offering pan is no-account."

"We don't need any goody-goody stuff in this town," Dub assented. His budding goatee wagged emphatically. "The first thing you know, Preach will be trying to shut down the saloon and the dance hall. They all do."

"We won't let him get that far," Nick chimed in. "Can't take any chances."

"We've already started on him." Harlo had a strangely mobile countenance. It was quick to advertise the emotions of its owner. "We let the air out of his tires. But that is mild compared to what we plan to do."

"Now, gentlemen," Boze said, quite businesslike, "we can't do anything criminal to land us in the hoosegow. I would have nobody to defend me."

"Aw," Harlo spoke up, "Dub's old man is the sheriff, and Dub would pull strings to get us out."

"No," Boze said majestically. "I wouldn't accept any strings that were pulled for me. The way I figure it, a real man stands on his own two feet and takes the rap for his actions. He doesn't hold to a mammy's apron, nor does he hide behind a pappy's greatcoat. Only sissies expect others to get them out of the tight they've cornered themselves into."

He saw that the boys liked his philosophy. It spoke of

independence, adulthood. "He's right, guys," Dub answered. "I'll back the backbone talk." It surprised Boze that Dub acquiesced to his takeover as though he was relieved to lay down the burden of making decisions. What was behind it all?

"Then we'll just have to take care not to get caught," Harlo suggested, "because we can't go pasty and let Preach change this town. It isn't our way."

"Our methods will take some thinking," Boze calculated, "but I believe we four can manage to get the results we need and keep our noses clean. All right. Everybody to our hidden cove at one o'clock to set the club in order and formulate a plan." The boys slouched away.

Boze had been blessed with a praying mother who respected God, His house, and His spokesman. Memory is an irascible companion, showing up at odd times. It put in its appearance now, and Boze knew he would have to find a way to protect the preacher from actual harm. He didn't agree with the young men's effrontery.

At the appointed place and the proper time, the three boys materialized. That was a good start. Boze had had time to think, and he was ready for them, every word weighed and measured.

"Now, gentlemen, since I am the eldest, I appoint myself as president of this order. All in favor say aye." The ayes were unanimous as Boze voted for himself.

"We need a name," Boze continued. "That bears careful thought. Every fraternity has a name for identity. What shall we call ourselves?"

"The Ambush Gang," suggested Nick. "With what we plan to do to Preach—"

"That's good but not powerful enough," Boze mused.

"Think some more. The name has to be right. It has to fit us."

"Army Gadders," offered Harlo, striving as young fellows will to cover his ignorance with a display of sententiousness. "Isn't that some tough end-of-the-world group mentioned in the Bible?"

"That's better," encouraged Boze. "Can anyone top that?" Dub's face was contorted in deep thought. "Dub? Any suggestions?"

"Holy Terrors."

To be diplomatic, Boze had to let one of the names stand. Dub had been their doyen, and his it should be. "Perfect!" shouted Boze. "All in favor of our club being named Holy Terrors raise your right hand." Four hands approved.

"Now, we need a treasurer. We'll have dues so we can pay fair and square for the supplies we need. I won't be able to give much money myself, but I could bum us up a lunch now and then. We will select our treasurer by secret ballot. Since I am president, I will not be eligible for the job. One cannot hold two offices.

"Nick, please pass your hat; mine has a hole in the top. Everybody go out and find your ballot: a pebble for Dub, a twig for Harlo, and a leaf for Nick. And make it quick. We can't chance discovery."

The lot was cast with four small rocks in Nick's hat. Dub had voted for himself. Since he was the most prosperous of the group, Boze conceded, the choice was probably a good one.

"A cardinal rule of the club is that everybody be trustworthy," reminded Boze. "We trust each other, and we believe in each other, no questions asked. We will neither delve into each other's past nor future. Agreed?"

They nodded.

"Now, one more item on the agenda." Boze squared his sloped shoulders that bore the weight of the old overalls. "Every clan has an initiation, or it isn't worth its salt. Initiations are always painful. We have to do something we detest. So I am assigning each of us to do one good deed before our next meeting. This will serve two purposes: to make us worthy of our name by opposite polarity and to fool the town into thinking that we are good guys in case we ever need allies."

"But that good-deed rule does not include toadying to Preach, does it, Boze? I say that is costing too much to get into the club," frowned Harlo. "If that is the rule, I'm pulling out now."

"It doesn't include Preach," assured Boze. "We will worry about what to do with Preach at our next meeting. We take one step at a time.

"I'll give you a hint about the initiation requirement. The old ladies are the best targets, men. Do a little good deed for them, and they will think the Holy Terrors are angels."

"Is that all we have to do?" Dub asked.

"Yes, that is our total assignment until we meet back here next Friday. You have an entire week to prove yourselves honorable members of the Holy Terrors."

"We'll do it," Nick said, shooting out a hard-muscled hand. "We will pass the test." He turned to go.

"Wait," ordered Boze. "We must have a proper adjournment. All in favor of dismissing the order of the Holy Terrors, state your position."

"Let us be dismissed," said Dub.

Like three fisherman's knots in the same rope, they left arm in arm, and Boze shuffled along behind. His mother would have been proud of him. He had steered the minds of the hoods away from tormenting the parson for at least a week.

Suddenly he was hungry. Where could he beg a good meal today?

CHAPTER 4

Maybelle

Brother Harry enjoyed a peaceful week. There were no chalked messages on his fenders, no name-calling when he walked down the street, and no broken windows at the church. For this he was grateful, and he entertained a hope that an end had come to his persecution. Regardless of what the pranksters did, however, he had made up his mind to stay. If ever a town needed a godly witness, this one did. Why allow three boys to close down a church?

He had received another message from the town's chief informant, the handwriting noticeably feminine. It had been slipped under his door, a longer and more detailed note this time. By reading it, he couldn't decide whether the monger was in the church or out. Mentally sorting through his members, he couldn't locate her among his group. His sheep, he hoped, were above such tripe.

The all-seeing eye's note said: *Your reputation is being irreparably damaged. You must never again be caught at the widow's house after dark. . . .* When had he stayed at Sister Allison's after dark? He was sure he hadn't! On it rambled: *Also, the consensus of the city is that Miss Hawksbury is much too young for you, along with the fact that her character has fallen under question more than once. If you value your calling, the two of you will not visit in her home alone. As pertaining to the only other available woman, Maybelle Davis, the wardens of righteousness find no objection to her at this point.*

Maybelle Davis. Her name was on his list for today. Should he decide to take a wife, she probably was his best candidate. When one was a public servant, general opinion did come into play, unfortunately. He would make an extra effort to be friendly to Maybelle when he called. Tucking some spice into his pocket to make sure he smelled good, he set out.

On that Thursday, Harry cut short his other visits so that he might spend more time with Maybelle. He would not go inside, of course, lest the gossiper condemn him. They would sit on the porch or under a tree, and he would perceptively learn what he could about the lady whom the town had chosen for him.

As he brought the automobile to a grating stop in front of the old maid's house, Brother Harry heard the loud and jerky notes of a piano. The playing continued without a pause as he got out of his car. Nearing the door, he received the full benefit of Maybelle's high, operatic voice as it trilled, "And I shall . . . the . . . vic-tor . . . beeeeeeeee. . . ."

Harry shuddered. How would one ever become accustomed to that wobbly singing? As for himself, he preferred plain music, a modulation easier on the ears.

He knocked, but Maybelle kept squawking out the miserable notes. He pounded harder, trying to ignore the ear abuse. "Miss Davis!" he called.

"Oh!" The pounding stopped. "Why, Parson Harry, what a pleasant surprise! Well, it is Thursday, isn't it, and your day to call? Please, do come in. If you don't mind, I will finish my song."

"Really, I would prefer a visit outside," Harry requested. "It is so pleasant out, and it is a policy of mine—"

"Well, certainly. As you wish, to be sure. It will be a delight to share your company inside or out, I'm sure. I will bring chairs. And I will make us some lemonade." A little girl admiring her array of dolls or Alexander the Great reviewing his regiments of soldiers might have been expected to indulge in a similar gesture of satisfaction.

She returned with refreshments. At least, she was passing the hostess test, Harry acceded. One gold star for her. A parson's wife must be able to entertain with dignity.

"I didn't know that you played an instrument," he mentioned when they were situated on the lawn. "No one told me."

"Oh, yes," she smiled archly, showing a set of large and crooked teeth. "I took lessons when I was in grammar school. The teacher claimed I had exceptional talent, and my father allowed I would find a need for my abilities down life's road. He predicted that I would marry either a parson or a bartender, and whichever I chose would appreciate my musical training. Of course, after I dedicated myself to the church, I knew that I would never yoke myself up with a bartender."

Dub sauntered by, and Maybelle gave him a cheery wave. "Do you know that young man?" she asked.

"That is the sheriff's son, is it not?"

"Yes, that's Mr. McIver's boy, and he is the nicest young man. He came by earlier in the week and asked if there was any little chore he might do for me, seeing as I was single and all. I told him I would like my piano moved from the back room to the front.

"He brought two of his friends, and they moved that heavy thing as if it were a match stick! Such charming fellows. And what muscles!

"I find it much more convenient to practice my music in the parlor. The back room was so crowded.

"Sister Hattie has been playing the pump organ at church since I was in pigtails. One day it occurred to me that she must be nearing a century old and that her arthritis wouldn't suffer her to play forever. Some of us younger ones should be preparing to step into the shoes of those who will soon be gone to their rewards. I know of no member of the church who could replace Sister Hattie other than myself."

"You can play the pump organ, too?"

"The octaves are the same."

"Oh, I didn't know."

"A bit of practice on the treadles and I shall have it mastered."

Harry's tongue was thick, but he tried to contribute to the dialogue. "My grandfather played a violin. I have his fiddle, but I don't know a measure of music."

"Oh, you must learn, dear parson! I love violin music. It has a witchery that is both propelling and ravishing! The mesmerizing rhythm, the sweeping melody, the capricious accents! Chromatic marvels! It would be a sin for you to leave the instrument unfulfilled. I can teach you to play."

"I'm not sure—"

"Oh, yes, yes. We can practice together."

"At the church?"

"Right here at my house."

"Someone might condemn—"

"Of course not. Everyone knows that I teach music. But no one would condemn you anyway, because we'd be working together for God."

This might be a way to become better acquainted with Miss Davis. "How old are you, Miss Davis, if the question isn't too personal?" How would he ever know if he didn't ask?

"I'm thirty-nine years, ten months, and fifteen days old. That makes me three years, two months, and eight days younger than you. Just right."

Harry's mouth dropped. "How did you know—?"

"Party lines, parson. They are the curse of our modern age. I chanced to lift the receiver while Miss Hawksbury and Sister Allison were in the midst of a verbal paragraph. They were discussing you. Sister Allison said you share a birth date with her six-year-old son, John. I remembered the exact month and day he was born. You will soon be forty-four."

"I will. What else did they say about me?"

"I hung up before I heard more. There are too many busybodies in this town as it is. The right hand always knows what the left is doing, plus both feet."

Harry laughed. His mind harked back to the note he'd found pushed under his door this morning, probably penned by one of the rumor spreaders Maybelle was alluding to just now. "A parson lives in a glass house," he said. "He has to be cautious."

"Unmarried parsons are always more susceptible to wagging tongues than married ones," said she. "That is one of the benefits of wedlock. People don't bother much with a man who has a pious wife."

Maybelle turned to face him, and a bright ray of sunshine hit her between the eyes like a revealing flash of lightning. She wasn't nearly as pretty as Fiona or even as fetching of face as the widow. In addition to unsightly teeth, she had limp, straw-colored hair and a long nose. But then, looks were just on the outside. The paint on his Ford did not determine its dependability; what was under the hood mattered.

"Why is it that you have never taken a wife, Brother Harry?" she asked bluntly. "That question has been of some preoccupation to the gossipers. They are whispering that you may have a skeleton in your closet."

Honesty was the safest route. "I hadn't the, er, freedom to marry earlier in life," he stammered. "My father went on to be with the Lord when I was a mere eleven years old, leaving me with a family to care for. I supported my mother, who had a lingering illness, until she passed away late last year."

Maybelle's pointed gaze was measuring him, making him uncomfortable. "Tell me about yourself, Miss Davis." He hoped to bait her away from any discussion of himself. If she didn't look away, he would suffocate!

"There isn't much to tell, really. I'm neither rich nor poor, fat nor skinny, young nor old, and I don't have children or a dog."

"I see." Harry's feelings were getting jumbled. Something between the lines of what she said troubled him.

"My greatest boon is my music, and there I shine. Even my name resounds with a beautiful melody: Maybelle. Don't you think so? Say it."

"Maybelle." The name tasted strange on his tongue.

"I think, parson, that you and I should become better acquainted. And in order to do that, you must come more often. Music lessons will be your perfect alibi."

Harry was having second thoughts. "I have a rather full schedule, but I will see what I can do."

"How about your very first lesson tomorrow?"

He had third thoughts. "My day is filled with appointments."

Maybelle made no attempt to disguise her disappointment at her disarranged plans. "Is Widow Allison on tomorrow's calendar?" she probed.

"No."

Maybelle smiled. "How about Fiona Hawksbury?"

"No."

Maybelle's smile broadened, showing all of her uneven teeth. With the most determined of efforts, Harry kept his legs from running to his vehicle to get away from that frightening smile, a smile that reminded him of a tigress that had just caught her prey.

Ghastly thoughts tumbled one on top of the other, swifter than he could count or sort them. As he drove away, as fast as the Ford would go, he imagined that he heard the rousing notes of the piano and a high, quivering voice trailing after him: "And I shall . . . the . . . vic-tor . . . beeeeeeeee. . . ."

CHAPTER 5

Recommendations

The Holy Terrors met again on Friday. Each had a good deed to report, hoping to pass the requirements of induction into the gang. Boze gave them an opportunity to tell what they had done so that the body might vote on their membership. If they had done anything of merit, he planned to grant approval.

Dub reported first. He had moved a piano for an old maid, enlisting the help of Nick and Harlo. "But, of course, that doesn't count on their record," he was quick to point out. The spinster had been so lavish with her thanks, he blushed, that he needed a bath to wash off the syrup. She had wanted him to stay to hear her play the miserable old instrument, he said, but he had begged off. He allowed that his good deed clause didn't cover concerts.

"You see," Boze pointed out, "now that you have been kind to her, she would stand for you against the devil himself. Let's vote on that deed, boys. Does Dub deserve acceptance by the Holy Terrors?"

"Aye," they chanted.

"And what did you do, Nick?" Boze stabbed a finger toward the next in line.

"I cut wood for Widow Allison's cook stove. I stacked it behind her house. You can go look if you don't believe me. Nobody saw me doing it, not even the kids. I hauled it in before they got up."

"We believe you, Nick," Boze said. "Honesty is a password in this order. What do you say, guys? Shall we admit him?"

"Aye."

"And you, Harlo?"

"I slopped Farmer Finley's hogs for him. He cut his hand on a piece of tin and was trying to do his work one-handed."

"What was his response?"

Harlo ducked his head. "Aw, he used such lofty words to describe me that I don't even want to repeat them. Hogwash, that's what they were."

"How do we vote, fellows?"

"Let him in."

"Then it is settled—"

"Now, whoa, Boze. Wait a minute." Dub held up his hand. "What did you do?"

"I was hoping you would ask," Boze grinned. "I did the most noble deed of all. It surpasses anything you could have thought of. In fact, I don't think a one of you would have had the gumption to try it."

"Tell it."

"I cleaned Preach's church for him. From stem to stern! Since we are Holy Terrors, I told myself, I will do something to uphold our namesake. And what is holier than a church? I washed the benches, polished the mourner's bench, and scrubbed the floors. Now is that going to extremes, or what? How are you going to vote? Am I in?"

They slapped him on the back. "The ultimate price!" they crowed. "You outdid all of us. You did what we would have detested the most. Bravo!"

"Then I passed?"

"Welcome to the Holy Terrors."

"And now that we have done our good deeds, we can put them behind us," suggested Harlo.

"Yes," agreed Boze, "but with our not-so-good deeds, we need to start slowly. If you land me in jail, you will have no president, and none of us will have any fun. I have a head full of great ideas, but they will all take time. We will institute only one prank a week for the first little while. That way, any fuss will have time to die down before the next project."

"What is on the docket for this week?" This came from Nick, the youngest and smallest of the group.

"We're going to take Preach's pretty little car for a joyride."

"Aw-right!" yelled Nick. "Say, you're a caper, Boze."

"What's the game plan?" Harlo asked, and the boys moved into a tight circle.

"We'll push the flivver away from his house in the morning before daybreak. We must make sure it is still dark; let's say five o'clock. Then when we are out of earshot, we will take a journey. I will drive, or we can take turns driving."

"I've always wanted to ride in a horseless carriage," blurted Nick. "What a plan! What a leader!" His immaturity showed in the boyish jig he danced.

43

"When we have had our fun, we will park the motor-car at Preach's church and split."

"Hurrah!" Dub's head bobbed. "If all Boze's projects are this much fun, we won't mind waiting a week between, will we boys?"

"Now. Did anyone remember to bring your dues?" Boze asked.

"I did," Dub responded. "I brought a dollar."

Boze leveled a gaze on him. "Is it your dollar fair and square, Dub? We won't allow any stealing or cheating for our dues. This is a man's club. A man earns his money honorably."

"It is mine," he replied, and his eyes were clear. "I sold some horses for Paw, and he paid me."

"I only have a nickel," Nick offered.

"That's okay. It's freewill," reminded Boze. "We don't want to make it hard on anyone."

"I have two bits," Harlo said, "and it's clean money."

"I have a dime." Boze fished the coin from the pocket of his overalls. "Sometimes people feel sorry for me and give me a little money. There are advantages to being a hobo."

The change was passed to Dub. "That makes one dollar and forty cents," he counted.

"A good start," cheered Boze. "The Holy Terrors are on solid financial ground."

"What will we spend it for?" Nick wanted to know.

"Whatever necessity requests."

"Whiskey?" twittered Nick.

"A real man doesn't tarnish his mind, his body, or his soul with strong drink," Boze spoke out. "This club is for real men only."

"How about a picnic? With a watermelon?"

"Now you're coming down my alley," Boze said.

"Where do you eat, Boze?" Dub asked, and his concern touched the hobo.

"Well, men, I was going to ask about some of the townspeople. Most folks will offer a hobo a bite to eat, but you three have lived here all your lives, while I haven't. Perhaps you could recommend a generous hand."

"Don't go to the Hawk's house!" warned Harlo.

"The Hawk?"

"Fiona Hawksbury. She lives in that big spread on the west edge of town with the fancy fence all around. She wouldn't give a bird a crumb in winter if the critter was starving to death."

"Yep. She invented stingy," nodded Nick.

"They say she has thousands of dollars in the bank," Harlo said. "But she squeezes a penny so tight the Indian on it squalls."

"She was the only child of a big cattle rustler," explained Dub. "Her paw died and left everything to her."

"She's had dozens of boyfriends," Harlo contributed, "and now she is after Preach. She'll have him trapped and strung up before the summer is over. You just hide and bide."

"She'll torment him more than ever we could," Dub said. "I'd rather be pistol-whipped than to be stuck with her for a wife."

"You haven't told me where to get food," reminded Boze dryly. "You've only told me where I can't get it."

Dub tugged at his goatee. "The best place would probably be Widow Allison's, don't you think, boys? She couldn't turn a mangy varmint away. And that woman can cook! I'd almost turn churchy on fifth Sundays when they have those dinners on the ground so as to get to eat her biscuits. Once when Maw was sick, the widow brought us some food. Man, it was scrumptious."

"And where does she live?" Boze asked.

"It's a shotgun house out south," answered Dub. "The next to the last on the left. It's not much of a place to look at, but it'll hold a welcome. She'll be likely to share dinner. She has three kids. John-John is the youngest, then there's Luther, and Louisa is the oldest. She's right fetching as girls go."

"Ooh! Dub's got a bonnie," taunted Nick. Then in a singsong voice, "A bottle of ink to make him stink, a bottle of wine to make him whine, and Louis-ah to kiss him all the time!"

Dub's fist doubled, and his brows bunched together angrily. He lunged at the smaller boy with all intentions of flattening his nose, but Boze caught his hand. "Fighting amongst ourselves is against club rules," he said authoritatively. "I, as president, reserve the right to expel scrappers from the order of the Holy Terrors."

He turned to Nick. "Nick, tell Dub you are sorry." Boze's good eye bored into Nick.

After a pause, Nick mumbled, "Sorry, Dub."

"Anywhere else to get grub?" Boze brought the crackling atmosphere back to normal.

"You might try Mrs. Farley's."

"Where—?"

"Away out by Washita River."

"Too far to walk."

"Or the old maid. She lives smack in the middle of town. Behind the general store. She's got a crush on Preach, too."

"Thanks," Boze said. "Mayhap one of them will favor an old hobo. And remember, guys, just before daylight we gather at Preach's house—"

"There's an old shed we can meet behind."

"Superb. Five o'clock. Meeting dismissed."

The boys disappeared, but Boze lingered. He made his way back to town, pondering. Was taking the parson's car a good idea?

CHAPTER 6

Reactions

Boze's empty stomach rumbled with hunger. He'd had no breakfast, and the thought of food spurred him on.

South . . . Next to last house . . . On the left . . . A widow with three kids . . .

Straightening his battered hat as a matter of habit, Boze knocked on the door and waited. "Mama!" informed a child's high-pitched voice. "It's a hobo with a blind eye!"

The widow came to the door, wiping flour-whitened hands on a threadbare apron. She stammered apologies for her child's rudeness.

"No offense, Mum," Boze appeased. "Children will be children. Could you spare a morsel of food to a hungry beggar?"

"I've never turned anyone away," smiled Mrs. Allison. "It always frights me that I might lose a chance to entertain angels unawares. If you will sit there in the porch swing, I will fix you up a nice feast."

"Much obliged, Mum." Boze sat down to wait, congratulating himself for finding a humanitarian soul.

Around the corner of the house came a mid-sized boy. "Hello," the boy said. "I'm Luther." He plopped down in the swing beside Boze. "I'm twelve."

"Lived here all your life?" Boze asked.

"Ever' bit of it," Luther said. "Never been anywhere else. It must be wonderful to travel on trains."

"It must be wonderful to have a home," countered Boze, "and good food."

"Yeah. My mama is the best cook in all the world," Luther nodded. "If I went on a train, I'd come back."

"A good idea," agreed Boze. "It isn't the fun it seems out there on those rails."

"Do you like to fish?" Luther asked.

"That's my favorite sport," Boze answered.

"My papa used to take me fishing before he went to war." Luther's words were pensive. "Sometime when you're coming through, would you take me fishing?"

"That would be up to your maw."

"I think I could talk her into letting me go." He glanced up at Boze, seeming to notice the eye patch for the first time. "What happened to your eye, sir?"

"Uh, well, I—"

The door opened, and the widow stepped out. "Here, mister. May God bless this food to the nourishment and strength of your body." It was almost like a benediction such as his mother used to give, and Boze bowed his head.

"Luther, run along now and let the man eat," exhorted the lady. "He's hungry."

Boze thought he had never tasted such delicious food. There were chitlins and fried potatoes. Dub hadn't exaggerated about the widow's biscuits. She'd filled one with butter and honey for his dessert.

When Boze was through, he wiped his mouth on the sleeve of his shirt. After a proper "thank you," he went back to Red Deer Creek for a spell of fishing, more or less precipitated by Luther's bringing up the subject. The air was warm and lazy with the sweet fragrance of grass and wildflowers. A late spring sun and a full stomach lulled him to sleep.

He had planned to catch a mess of fish and bake them over an open fire for his supper, but the perch didn't cooperate. The wind was from the east, a direction (he'd heard) when the fish bite least. He supposed that he would be obliged to go into town to bum another meal, but it didn't seem quite right to impose upon the widow again.

Perhaps he would try the old maid whom the boys had told him about. She lived behind the general store, they said. Now what had the boys told him about her? Nothing that he could remember except that she had her heart set on the preacher. It seemed that if Preach didn't run fast, someone would catch him.

He stopped short at the old maid's door. Had she company? He could hear her talking—and loudly—to someone. "Whatever you say, Fiona. I am going to give him violin lessons! It is his wishes. Yes, Fiona, I am a very capable music teacher, thank you. And, oh, I can hardly wait! When I show him how to hold the bow properly, I will practically have to hug him—"

Boze knocked.

"Pardon me, Fiona, but I have someone at my door. Perhaps it is Brother Harry coming for his music lesson." The earpiece clicked into its receptacle, and the sound of footsteps brought a woman with too many teeth to the door.

"Oh," she drew back. "I—I thought you were— That is, why did you come here?"

She was neither kind nor unkind, friendly nor unfriendly. The tenor of her question gave Boze hope. "Mum, I was passing this way, and I wondered if you could spare a bite to eat for a poor man?"

"My good parents taught me that one should work for his living," said the lady tersely. "I don't give anything to a tramp."

Boze turned away.

"But wait!" she ordered. "I have some work that you can do. If you will deliver a note for me, I shall give you some milk and a freshly baked muffin."

"Most gladly, mum," answered Boze.

"Then sit. I'll bring the goodies, and while you eat, I shall prepare my message."

"Yes, mum."

The muffins were good, but they didn't hold a candle to the widow's biscuits. They tended to stick to the roof of Boze's mouth when he tried to swallow. *But I reckon beggars can't be choosers*, he chuckled to himself.

The lady took an extraordinarily long time to write the note she wished delivered. Boze fidgeted and patted a foot encased in an oversized shoe. He wished she would hurry.

He was nodding off when she returned. "Here it is," she said. "It goes to the parson's house. If you find him at home, deliver it to him personally, but take care not to let him know who sent it. If he is out visiting, slide it under the door. He lives on the east side of town, the only house with a stone-lined walkway to the front door. His Ford will be there unless he is away."

"Yes, mum."

"And you dare not open the envelope."

"Oh, no, mum. My maw taught me better."

"Now anytime you are coming back through on the train, I will give you a treat for playing postman for me."

"Nice of you, mum."

Boze hurried to the parson's house and pushed the note under his door. He wondered if it was a love note. A small temptation to look at the message seized him, but he did not yield to that urge.

The muffin didn't quite fill the hollow spot in Boze's middle. He would like to have something more substantial. Harlo had mentioned "the Hawk," vowing she would not give a thirsting man a drop of water to cool his parching tongue. But Harlo might be wrong. What harm could come of trying?

To the big spread on the west edge of town, Boze walked. The place was impressive; a veranda was muscled up by white columns. By the front window stood a table with two big ferns in brass holders. What would it be like to live in a grand house like that? What would it be like to have plenty of money?

As he went through the gate of the picket fence, a bell jangled, announcing his arrival. A tall young woman came to the door, her hair piled high on her head. She was strikingly beautiful! Her skirts swished about her; she might have walked out of a storybook.

Then from behind her hurled a ball of flying fuzz. "Sic him, Frazzles!" urged the woman. "Bite him!"

Before Boze knew what had happened, the fur ball

had him by a trouser leg. A wicked growl rumbled deep in his throat. "M-mum," Boze pleaded. "Please call your dog off. I won't harm you or your animal. I promise!"

"Get off my property, you scum!" she lashed at him with the blade of her tongue, her face filled with hate. "You are filthy. You are a bad man. I hate hoboes! They are evil!" She flicked a speck of invisible dust from her immaculate dirndl.

"I—I just wanted—food."

"I wouldn't give you a teaspoon of Frazzles's dog food!" she screamed. "Get back on your train, and go to the poor farm where you belong, you wretched drifter. My dog knows when a man is dangerous. He can read human character in whatever garb a man appears. Why, he loves the parson."

"Mum, believe me, I wouldn't harm—"

"Go. Get! Scram!" With her lips pressed tightly against her teeth, her words flowed like the hiss of a snake. She reached down, picked up a stick and came at him, reviling him in a muddy torrent of verbiage.

"Yes. I'll go, mum. I'll be glad to go. Just get your hound to turn loose."

"He's no hound. He's a precious poochie. Come Frazzles. You did a wonderful job, you sweet thing. You protected Fiona." She pulled him to herself and hugged him.

Boze left the yard in a run. He had never been treated worse. The boys hadn't exaggerated about this one, either. What a shame it was for such a comely young lady to have such a biased view of a man who only asked for a handout.

Even hoboes have a sense of pride. Boze decided he

would rather perish than ask alms from that manicured hand again. And the dreadful mutt . . . He shuddered. Only by the mercies of his high-topped shoes was he spared the animal's snapping teeth.

CHAPTER 7

A Short Ride

In the moldy darkness, Boze stationed himself behind the listing shed to await the arrival of the Holy Terrors. It was a quarter to five, and he occupied the most hidden spot on the property, out of view of the road and out of view of the house. Would the boys show up at this impious hour, a time when night revelers were just beginning their sleep? The joke might be on him!

Concentrating on the buzz of a mosquito and slapping about to exterminate the insect, Boze didn't hear Dub's soundless approach. He jumped when Dub touched his shoulder. "The others are coming," Dub whispered. "We're lucky. We have a cloud cover this morning."

"Did you sleep well?" Boze asked.

"I did."

"I didn't," admitted Boze. "I was excited. Or nervous. Or something. What if we get caught?"

"You're not going chicken on us, are you?"

"Oh, no," responded Boze quickly. "Nothing like that. We're going to have a grand time."

"Unless we awaken Preach."

"We won't."

Nick and Harlo joined them. "We're ready for adventure." They rubbed their hands together. "Let's go."

Four silent figures moved through the dimness to the radiator of the car. Silently, they eased it backward to the open street. Then they got behind it and pushed it forward until they were well away from the parson's house. "Now," instructed Nick, "we have to crank it."

"Wait," Boze pulled Nick's arm back when he reached for the handle. "This is the most dangerous part. You have to pull up. Don't wrap your thumb around the crank in case she decides to kick back. Like this, see?" the hobo demonstrated, moving to one side to let the boy take over.

"How do you know so much about it?"

"He cranked the train," razzed Harlo.

"And I wasn't born yesterday," reminded Boze. "Go ahead and start it, Nick."

Nick yanked so powerfully that the engine leapt to rollicking life. "I did it!" he bragged. "I did it on the first try."

"Get in!" Boze yelled above the awful racket. He slid into the driver's seat, gripping the wooden steering wheel. The vehicle shook so that the quartet looked palsied. Dub and Harlo tumbled into the rumble seat.

"I don't know but what I would choose a mule and a saddle," Harlo groused. "I may not have any teeth left."

"This is better than teeth," Nick yelled.

"Here we go!" warned Boze. "Hold your hats."

"What about the headlamps, Boze? We can't see where we are going."

"We'll light them when we are well out of town."

"Where are we going?"

"Nowhere in particular. Just riding for the fun of it."

They bumped along Main Street, gaining speed as they went. Dogs barked and cows bellowed, indignant that their sleep was disturbed, but the town slumbered on. "If anybody wakes up, they'll just think the parson got called out early," Dub said.

A mile out, they started up a hill, savoring the thrill of the sport. The car gave a burp, followed by a few shakes, and died. "Uh-oh," Boze said. "Problems. Jump out and chock the wheels, boys, so we don't roll backward. I'll see if I can find the problem." Dub and Harlo exploded from the rumble seat like wads from a double-barreled shotgun. They put rocks behind the tires.

Boze walked around and around the car, striking matches for light. "Nothing seems amiss. There's oil. There's spark. There's water in the radiator. Obviously, we are out of fuel. Without gasoline, motors won't run."

"What will we do?" Nick queried.

"There's a can tied to the bumper here," noted Boze. "One of us will have to go wake up Mr. Winfield and get him to fill this can if we plan to ride this morning. In fact, if we plan to go far, we ought to fill the tank. Did you bring the club's money, Dub?"

"I don't go anywhere without it."

"It may take a dollar to fill it up."

"A good investment," Harlo approved. "I vote to fill it to the brim."

"Aye," chimed Nick and Dub.

"And who will go for the gasoline?"

"Nick and I will go," offered Harlo.

Dub tossed him the silver dollar. "Keep the change for your trouble," he said, shooing them away.

"Sometimes I get tired of those two," Dub soughed to Boze. "They are so immature."

"But we'll have patience with them," Boze said. "Time most often cures immaturity."

"If it wasn't for you, I wouldn't even be in this club."

"You aren't having a good time?"

"How can anyone have a good time with babies?"

Something was eating at Dub. "Stay with me, Dub, and we'll make men of these boys."

"I don't know if they're worth our trouble."

Nick and Harlo chuffed back, japing. "Old man Winfield wanted to know what we needed with gasoline this time of the morning."

"What did you tell him?"

"We told him we were going to pour it on ant beds to kill the ants."

"Next time don't lie," censured Boze. "That's against the rules."

The first faint pencilling of dawn was tinting the upper sky before they got the car going again. "We'll have to hurry," Boze prompted. "We don't want to get caught with this flivver. We'd have some tall explaining to do."

"The plans are to abandon it at the church?"

"Right."

"But what about the gasoline we put in?" Nick asked. "It doesn't seem fair—"

"That's part of the grand trick," Boze pointed out. "When we took it, it was empty. When Preach finds it—and learns that there is gasoline in the tank—maybe he'll think an angel kidnapped it!"

"Oh, ha, ha!" Nick sniggered. "Won't that be funny?"

"But how will we ever know how Preach reacts?"

"We'll put Dub on the roof of the church to watch Preach," Boze said. "I'm too clumsy to climb the roof myself, and I'm willing to hear secondhand reports from our treasurer. When we gather at the creek for our weekly business meeting, we'll hear the tale then."

"We didn't have a very long ride," complained Nick, his tanned, boyish face that had never known a razor twisted in annoyance and exasperation. "And I wanted to drive."

"Hobo's luck," Boze concluded. "Who would have thought the horseless boasted nothing but fumes when we picked her up? To the churchyard we go, boys, before the sun gives our secret away."

He drove to the church grounds. "Now, Dub, it is up to you to bring us the yarn."

CHAPTER 8

The Widow

Brother Harry's salary of three dollars failed to show up in the pan that week. The love of money might be the root of all evil, he told himself, but currency never stayed in his pockets long enough to put forth roots. His vehicle was running on fumes and his body on water gravy. How much farther either of them would go, it would be idle to estimate.

This morning he wrestled with a button, thread, and a needle. He hadn't been able to find any white thread in the sewing basket, a repository that had belonged to his mother. An ecru color would have to serve his purpose.

The loose button was the one that fastened his collar. It would be hidden behind his bow tie anyway. What mattered the color that anchored it?

One advantage of having a wife would be that he would have someone to replace the buttons on his shirts. Besides ironing, it was his most dreaded chore. He could ask the widow to do it for him, of course, but that would be imposing on her.

He jabbed the needle clumsily through the holes in the button. There were four holes, and Brother Harry had a terrible time remembering which way the thread should go. He finally decided to make a square path of the thread, going from one buttonhole to the next all the way around. That seemed the best way to secure the bothersome fastener.

When the job was completed, he finished dressing so that he might make his pastoral calls. The Widow Allison was on his list today, and he found himself glad. Fiona Hawksbury wasn't, and he found himself even gladder. As he started out, he saw a smudged envelope stuffed beneath the front door. He picked it up, turned it over, and looked at it. There was no address, no hint as to who sent it. Quickly, he tore it open.

I am looking out for your welfare, the note said. *It would be best for you to find someone else to iron your shirts. The town is talking, and so is the widow. There are many other women who can wash and iron without your jeopardizing your good name by leaving something so personal as a shirt in the home of an unattached woman. Servants of God must take great care not to put themselves in a bad light. Most believe in your innocence, but a few are beginning to ask questions.* The note was not signed.

Brother Harry laid the page on the table. His feelings for the widow were still new to him, a sweet mood shut away in his heart. It was an unpleasant shock to find that busy tongues were already bringing it into the open. *But,* his stubborn defenses argued, *why should it matter who fries my shirts?*

He walked out to find that his car was missing; he had

no doubts as to who had taken it. "Bless them," he said. "The gas tank was empty."

When visiting, the parson always took his Bible. Absentmindedly, he had left it at the church. He made his way there to retrieve it. Sitting directly in front of the sanctuary was his Model T.

"Well, glory be!" he said. "If it isn't my car! Left sitting right here in a good place. Whosoever took it must have run out of fuel ere they got away. Poor dears. I could have told them it was nigh to bone dry. It takes gasoline, and it takes money to run a road machine." He was talking aloud, a practice of his.

"If I had some money, I could buy a can of ethyl from Mr. Winfield." He removed the cap from the tank and peered in. Stepping back, he scratched his head. "Do I see a flash down there?"

He looked about him and found a stick, which he poked into the gas line. "Ah, a tank full of water," he said. "They've watered it again."

He lifted the stick to his nose and sniffed. "Wa— No, it isn't water! It is pure gasoline. Hallelujah! But how did it get there? Did a holy angel put it there?" Raising his eyes toward heaven, he was sure that he saw a movement atop the church.

"If that is you, holy angel, thanks!"

The engine fired, and he was off with a clatter and a flourish, forgetting his empty pockets. God had supplied his needs.

To the widow's house he went, unheeding of his crooked tie or hair gone askew. She met him at the door, wearing a cotton calico dress with a full skirt almost to her ankles. She was as much in disarray as he, giving witness that she had not expected him this early. His previous calls had been after noon.

"Blessings, Brother Harry," she smiled, undaunted. "Do come in." Her gray-blue eyes held his with a touch of reserve. Thick mahogany hair laced with gray drifted from its rat and straggled about her neck. Age lines sprouted at the corners of her eyes, and a bit of girth gathered at her waist. Everything about her said, "I'm past forty and not ashamed to show it because I have three wonderful reasons why." Those three reasons lingered around the breakfast table in homemade feed-sack clothes that were starched and ironed to perfection. The room with all its furniture and rugs had a comfortable atmosphere.

"Hurry, children," she urged. "You must not be late to school."

She turned to him. "Have you had breakfast, Brother Harry?"

"Well, I—" His mouth watered at the sight of the biscuits.

"Sit down and have a biscuit with some butter and molasses," she insisted. "The children and I are finished, and there are plenty left."

He sat down and devoured the last four biscuits while the widow helped the children with their last-minute preparations. "I always pray with my children before they depart, Brother Harry," she said softly. "I station angels about them. Will you pray with us?"

"Gladly," he answered.

"But, Maw, we'll be late," Luther objected. "I don't like being late. Everyone stares at me."

"Better late and angeled than on time and unguarded," she said.

"I'll drive the children to school in my car," offered Brother Harry and then wondered why he had said it. He was asking for a peck of trouble from the town gossip should she discover his noble deed.

"Will you drop back by?" asked the widow.

He hesitated. What excuse could he use to return?

"I have your shirts ready."

"I'll pick them up."

The first paternal feelings ever to stir in the parson's breast assaulted him when tiny John turned to thank him for the transportation. "You're nice like my paw would have been," he said. "Paw would have brung us to school." His smile released the power of a surprising pair of dimples, and Brother Harry thought the pound of gristle inside his chest might stop beating then and there.

Back at the widow's house, he would not go inside but stood at the door, shifting from foot to foot. "You have well-trained children," he commented. "The youngest thanked me properly for the ride."

"John-John," she smiled, and he turned his head away lest she, too, break out in those breath-stopping dimples. "That's just like him. I call him John-John because he is twice as precious as any other boy named John. He was a baby when I . . . lost his father, and he has been a great comfort to me. Jonathan thought the sun rose and set in Baby John."

Speech left Harry stranded on a tongue-tied shore. It suddenly dawned on him that he had no money to pay Grace Allison for the ironing. His ears burned with embarrassment.

"Uh, I'll have to ask for credit on the shirts," he stammered. "My apologies. The tithe hasn't come in yet, and—"

She waved his worry away. "I have no wants. God sent an angel to cut some wood for me, and I have plenty of kerosene for the lamps."

"God sent angels to fill my tank with gasoline, too," Brother Harry seconded, "else I'd be afoot."

"How is your garden coming on?" she asked, stabbing at a conversation.

"Tomatoes are abloom," he said.

"Mine, too," she said.

"I'm having a few radishes."

"Me, too."

"I found one little cucumber yesterday."

"Cucumbers grow fast. Almost overnight. That one you found will likely be ready to eat tomorrow."

"They grow that fast?"

"Yes, sir."

"That's good."

"Oh, before I forget, Brother Harry, Miss Maybelle Davis called while you were driving the children to school. She wants you to drop by while you are out, please."

Harry's stomach gave a lurch. Miss Maybelle . . . The woman the whole town wanted him to marry . . . She wasn't on his list today.

He turned to leave the widow's house. "One question, please, Brother Harry."

He faced her. "Yes?"

"An old hobo came by my house this week. Luther took up with him, and the bum has offered to take my boy fishing—"

"But Sister Allison! You don't know the man!"

"That's true, and I had some reservations. But Luther

68

misses his father so badly I am beginning to weaken. Most of the railroad hoboes are harmless, aren't they?"

"Most of them, yes. But we cannot take any chances."

"You meet with many of the itinerants from the train, don't you?"

"Often, yes."

"Would it be too much to ask that you watch for this one? His name is Boze. He said he would be back."

Harry chuckled. "His name might be Boze this week and Moze the next. But if you will describe him to me—"

"He won't be hard to spot. He has a patch over one eye."

"One eye is blind?"

"I couldn't tell you, sir. Luther wanted to ask what happened to his eye, but I told him that wasn't polite."

"Anything can happen on the boxcars."

"He also has a scar on his cheek."

"I'll keep a lookout for the man."

CHAPTER 9

A Dread Prospect

The list. Brother Harry decided he needed to rearrange his call list. It had become too predictable. Each of his members knew what day he would be where. That included Fiona.

Fiona Hawksbury had it down to a fine art. She was always waiting, beribboned and curled, with cinnamon tea and scones prepared for a tea party. The reception was for herself, Brother Harry, and the pesky dog. Not that Brother Harry didn't like tea and scones. He didn't like . . . the dog.

The frown in his mind had reached his face by the time he arrived at Maybelle Davis's house. Maybelle had called the widow's number and had requested that he visit. What could the old maid want today?

She was pounding her ear-splitting music when he parked his vehicle. That the keys could endure such blows he considered a miracle. Her treble voice quavered, "He is . . . all . . . the world . . . to . . . meeeee. . . ."

Harry could see her through the screen door, her hair

coiled into a thin, snaky tube. She whirled about at his knock. "Oh, Parson Harry, you always catch me at my practicing. But someday you will be glad I can enhance your ministry with my talents."

"Uh, perhaps so."

"Not everybody is musically inclined. Widow Allison told you that I called?"

"Yes." Her discerning look made him fidget. "I was there to get my laundry." Why must he forever offer explanations? When he chose to pick up his shirts was his own business.

Maybelle pinioned him with eyes possessed of a feverish light. "Widow Allison is such a busy woman and has three rambunctious kids. I'm sure it must be a struggle for her to find the time for extra laundry. In fact, she hinted as much. I have no children and plenty of free evenings. I will be happy to do your laundry without charge."

A savings of a dollar a month. "The money helps the widow with her expenses."

"She told you that?"

"No, but—"

"She gets a nice war pension. Don't listen to her poor-mouthing. If the truth were known, she probably gets more than the rest of us. With the exception of Fiona, of course."

"I like Sister Allison's work." Why was he arguing?

"Well, at the least, I could save you some time by collecting your shirts for you and having them here when you come for your violin lessons."

"Violin lessons?"

"It is time that we get started on the violin. The whole

congregation became terribly excited when I told them I would be teaching you to play. They know that music will command a larger crowd. Why, no one in this town plays a violin! Think what an attraction it will be!" She grew animated. "Ah, the violin! Violin music affects the emotions. It moves people. It produces the world's most evanescent melody!" Her eyes became large, owl-like.

"I haven't the time—"

"Oh, but you must make time for such an important undertaking. A violin-playing parson's position is virtually nailed down. Every church in the state will try to take you from us when they hear about it. But they shan't have you. Oh, no!"

Was she trying to puff his ego, or was it the truth? "How long will it take to learn?"

"That depends upon how often you can come for classes. The more frequently you can schedule a class, the sooner you will master the instrument."

"And the duration of each lesson?"

"At least an hour. That is, with a break every quarter. One's mind must have time for absorption. Here's something else to consider: The closer together the instructions, the more you will retain. If there are long lapses between classes, one tends to forget what one learned in the previous lesson, and the mastery will take longer."

"I fear that I cannot afford the lessons."

"Oh, dear parson, I shall not charge you! I will consider my time and efforts a contribution to the cause of God. It will become my mission, my calling."

"The—the town might talk. Someone is watching me, and with us in the house together—just you and I—and both unmarried—"

"Aw, pshaw!" she scorned. "This is different. I have given music lessons since I was graduated from the academy. Nobody will think a thing about it! In fact, I have already talked it around, and the entire community is in favor of it. How about having our first appointment tomorrow?"

"Well, I—"

"Fiona Hawksbury is on your schedule for tomorrow, isn't she?"

"Yes."

"She doesn't need visiting. I'll call and tell her that you aren't coming."

"I'll inform her myself."

"You usually call on her at one o'clock on Thursdays, don't you?"

"Usually."

"If you could be here at five past one, I will be ready to begin."

"What if I am not an apt learner?"

"With time and practice, anyone can accomplish his goals."

"Actually, I—"

"The secret of success is not to give up. One must not become discouraged with the first few lessons. One day everything will click, and you will bless the world with heavenly harmony!"

"I—"

"Thursday. We must put it off no longer. One-oh-five. Please be prompt; I haven't any tolerance with tardiness."

Brother Harry went home distressed. He had no desire to play the violin, quite certain that no native ability resided in his brain or in his fingers. Yet Maybelle said his church members wished him to be a musician. The crowds would increase, and that might mean a raise in pay. Glorious thought.

He lifted the violin case from the lid of the trunk and blew off the dust. The old instrument might have a broken string; that would liberate him. It would spare him the agony of Maybelle's dreaded lessons or, at the least, postpone them. But upon close examination, Harry found all the strings intact, the bow in its compartment, and a chunk of resin in a padded niche of black felt. He was doomed.

On Wednesday, he recalled his promise to the widow to check on the hobo. When the train came in with its rush and roar, raining cinders as it rolled to a grinding halt, he was there to meet it. A bedraggled hobo alighted. Harry didn't have the money to provide lunch for him, so he simply visited, offering friendship.

"Do you have a traveling buddy who has a blind eye?" he asked. "He wears an eye patch."

"No, pa'son," the man drawled. "Hain't met him, I reckon. What's his name?"

"Boze."

"Boze?" Again he shook his head. "Not on my train. Do you need me to fetch him a word if I see him?" he offered. "About his family, mayhap?"

"No, I was inquiring for a friend," Harry said. "Nothing important. And you have an invite to my church if you Sunday here."

"I'll be bumming on down the line," the hobo said. "I got off here for a stretch and a drink of water." He hurried back to the train.

That night, sleep eluded Harry. He had a multitude of

worries on his mind. Luther needed a friend, a father figure. But a hobo? As a pastor, it fell his responsibility to
provide emotional support for the young.

A new and exciting plan struck him. Why not arrange
a fishing trip for all the boys in his church? Their moth-
ers could pack lunches for them, and they could spend a
whole day at the Washita River. He was sure that he could
fit all the smaller ones into his car if the larger ones could
ride the fenders. He would sit John-John right beside him.

Somewhere in the grand plans intruded the thought of
tomorrow's violin lesson. He dreaded it as one dreads
changing the dressing on a wound, wishing he could put
it off a little longer.

He tumbled his bed into a terrible disorder, trying to
figure a way out of his quagmire, but could find no exit.
A season of repose could not have been more unsympa-
thetic. The interval between the last evening songs of the
birds and their first cries at daybreak was a span of night
without content, only stark blackness.

CHAPTER 10

Birthday Celebration

The Holy Terrors met on Friday. Nick tossed out a penny for the dues, Harlo a nickel, and Dub a dime. They now had fifty-six cents. "I hope we don't waste this like we wasted the dollar on gasoline," grumbled Nick.

"Yeah, you put in a whole penny," shot Dub. "If anybody has a right to gripe, it is I. Do you hear me griping?" After he let the comment sink in, Dub resumed, "I thought not. Then close your trap. I am the treasurer."

Boze gave Dub a "that's enough" look then dismissed the potential fracas by pulling out a sack of cookies he had collected for delivering another message to Preach's place. "My contribution," he piped. "I might just put in my application to be the mailman. Every time I go by the old maid's to beg a bite, she sends a sealed-up letter to Preach and pays me with goodies."

"She's probably sweet on Preach," said Harlo.

"She is," confirmed Dub. "That's common knowledge around town."

"Do you think Preach knows it?" Nick asked.

"If he doesn't, he's blind and dumb," Dub said.

"Or dead," was Harlo's comment.

"He isn't dead!" Dub forgot his bur and danced around. "Let me tell you about my perch on the roof of the church."

"Tell it. We're itching to hear," Boze urged. "We'll waive the minutes of the last meeting and go directly to the report we've all been eagerly waiting to receive. Dub, did the Holy Terrors score another success?"

"We did!" He slapped his knee in raucous laughter. "It was the funniest thing. Preach talks to himself, you know. He decided we had run dry of gasoline right there in the face of the church, and he was wishing he had some money to buy fuel from Mr. Winfield's pump. Why, he turned both pockets wrongside out looking for a single coin, but he had no luck.

"Then he peered in the gas tank, thinking we had filled it up with water again like we did before. He got a stick and ran it down in the tank. Then—oh, it was price-less!—he smelled the stick."

"Smelled it?"

"Yes. And when it reeked with gasoline fumes, he jumped back like that stick had bitten him. 'Hallelujah!' he bellowed. 'It is pure juice from heaven. A holy angel put it there!' Those were his exact words. Boys, did we fool him this time! It was well worth our dollar!"

They shook hands all around. "Perfect!" praised Boze. "You guys are making superb Terrors. Shall we torment someone else this week? I suggest that you three could waylay me as I am going to deliver the old maid's letter. That would torment her."

"No, no!" Nick insisted. "Preach is too much fun. He's so simple."

"But I think we ought to give him a rest."

"No rest for the righteous," Nick said.

"Then what can we do without landing me in the slammer?" Boze asked. "I haven't a hankering to dry-rot behind bars."

"Let's pull up his fancy little garden," Harlo suggested. "Without food, he will get willing to leave town all the sooner."

Boze's mind went into gear. Once more, it selected this moment to remind him of his mother, her respect for church, the parson, and God. He couldn't let these boys rob a town of a clergyman to marry and to bury its residents. Again, he must make them victims of his own inspiration.

"That's too easy," Boze said, talking deliberately but—quite separately—thinking fast.

"What do you mean?"

"Anybody can pull up plants. We, as Holy Terrors, strive for new ways to draw attention to our mischief. There is a better way."

"Name it."

"We will plant onions all over his garden so that everything that grows will taste like onions."

"And smell like onions," added Dub. "When he opens his mouth at church, his group will hit the back wall!"

"And we'll let him think it was the devil's doings."

"Where will we get the onions?" asked Harlo.

"Dumbo, they grow all over the place out here!" was Dub's retort. "Wild onions. All we need is some elbow grease."

"Tonight we plant onions," Boze said. "We should have some moonlight. And be careful not to touch or

79

break a tender vine in the garden, boys. You, Harlo, plant around the radishes if there are any. Nick, you take the cucumbers. Everybody has cucumbers. Dub will have the peppers or squash, and I will sow among the tomatoes. We'll share in the rest of the garden. Remember, we must put onions everywhere!"

"Then shall we put a watchdog out to see the apostle when he spies his new crop?" questioned Nick.

"Why not?"

"I want to be the spy this time," Nick said. "I'll sit in a tree."

"Shall we cast a vote, boys? All in favor of appointing Nick as our spy, say aye," Boze coached.

"Aye."

"Aye."

"Aye."

"Aye." Nick gave himself a strong vote.

"Okay. Tonight we will work. We will meet here to dig onions just before dark. We will leave them in clumps with a little dirt around the roots and hurry them to Preach's garden. Everyone knows their section. Nick will have us a report next Friday. The Holy Terrors are dismissed."

Boze headed for town, giving himself accolades. He didn't know how much longer he could divert the gang from actually harming the parson, but he would play it by ear. So far, so good. The boys had been pliable enough, making suggestions that bore easy revision. He hoped his luck continued.

Nearing town, his stomach growled. Hunger pangs cramped his belly. He dare not go back to the Hawk's place lest the mutt of a dog attack him again. To be so small, the mongrel was quite vicious. And to be so pretty, the lady snarled, too. He had already delivered the mail, so his chances for a bequest at the old maid's door weren't favorable.

That left the widow. It was a shame to hit her up this often, but for strength to plant dozens and dozens of onion sprouts tonight, he had to have nourishment. He limped toward her house.

Luther answered the door. "Maw, it is my friend, Boze," he called. "May he have supper with us?"

"Why, certainly, Luther," she answered from the kitchen.

"Come on in." Luther held the door wide. A marvelous aroma filled the house.

"Maw is cooking a cake," explained the young man. "Today is John-John's birthday. He is seven. Maw says seven is God's number, and John-John is God's gift."

"Oh, then I won't stay." Boze backed away.

"Oh, please stay and celebrate with us," begged Luther. "It will be special with you here. We never have guests except the parson, and he has only sat at our table once. We get lonesome for visitors."

It was a most pleasant evening. Boze had a penchant for carving in his idle moments, and he had whittled out a whistle from mesquite wood. He fished it from his pocket and gave it to the little boy for his birthday.

"Oh, thank you, sir!" the child rejoiced, and the light in his eyes brought a lump to Boze's throat.

After supper, Boze played a game of marbles with the boys on the worn linoleum floor while the widow and Louisa washed the dishes. He almost felt a part of the family.

The telephone rang, bringing the widow from the dishpan to answer it. Boze could only guess at the caller's motives. "Hello, Maybelle. . . . No, Brother Harry didn't mention it to me. . . . Really, Maybelle, I don't mind ironing his shirts. . . . If the parson prefers that you iron them, that is fine. . . . No, dear. . . . I didn't ask him to tote the children to school in his horseless. He offered to do so. . . . I see nothing inappropriate about it. . . . I am not trying to impress the parson. . . . Listen, Maybelle, may I call you back later? Today is John-John's birthday, and we are celebrating. . . . No, I did not invite the parson. . . . Yes, I know it is his birthday, too. . . . You might check at the church. . . . Goodbye, Maybelle."

"That was Brother Harry's violin teacher," volunteered Luther. "Likely she is ready to give him another lesson." His face became wistful. "I would love to play the fiddle, but I haven't an instrument on which to practice or the money for classes. I most nigh think I could learn on my own without a teacher. I can hear the notes in my head."

It was almost dark before Boze remembered the onion planting. "Oh, I must go," he hurried toward the door. "I have overstayed my visit."

The Holy Terrors would be waiting for him.

CHAPTER 11

First Lesson

Brother Harry had planned to plant some onions but hadn't gotten around to it. Then suddenly, two extraordinary things showed up in the patch: onion plants everywhere and a white envelope addressed to him.

Parson, the letter poured out its stream of rebuke, *you have stepped out of line again. We know that you are naive and (hopefully) innocent, but the citizens of Roberts County cannot continue to tolerate questionable actions on your part. The reference is to your transporting the widow's three children to school in your vehicle. The deed, though possibly well meant, has occasioned strong murmurs of disapproval.*

However, a point in your favor was reported to us by Miss Maybelle Davis. She states that you are withdrawing your employment of the widow in the matter of your ecclesiastical shirts. Preferring a lady never wed to do your laundry is a choice of profound wisdom.

Also to your credit is your interest in advancing

your pastoral effectiveness by incorporating music into your ministry. A parson who does not expand upon his aptitude will soon find himself a parson without a church.

We are glad to know that you are pulling away from the widow as well as the wealthy Miss Hawksbury, who plays her hand for any single male who moves to our area. Such a woman is mentioned in the Proverbs of Solomon. —The Informant

Brother Harry folded the letter into a square and put it in his pocket. Then he drove to Miss Hawksbury's house to inform her of his change of plans. She peeked through a tiny crack in the door to see who was there.

"Oh, Brother Harry," she sighed. "It is you. I thought it might be that dreadful old hobo again. Frazzles detests hoboes. But do let's talk."

"Not today, Miss Hawksbury."

Fiona didn't take the canceling of her visit from the parson kindly. "Frazzles will not understand, Brother Harry," she remonstrated. "Frazzles looks forward to your calls. Believe it or not, he knows the exact day of the week and hour of the day to expect you. He will interpret your abrupt departure as abandonment."

"But I have an appointment for a violin lesson," explained Harry. "The church members wish me to learn to play. Miss Davis is my teacher, and she insists that I be prompt."

"Miss Davis, Miss Davis," taunted Fiona with an air of condescension. "Maybelle is no more a music teacher than I am a lion tamer for the circus! Have you ever heard her play?"

"Uh, yes, but—"

"Her rhythm is off, her notes sour, and her pianissimo tragic. Why should anyone want to learn from her? I could teach you more in five minutes than you will learn from her in a year!" With scorn worthy of two marks of exclamation, she tossed her head, making the springs of brunette curls bob up and down.

"The church has requested—"

"Pooh! We don't care whether you play the violin or not. Such scritchy-scratchy sounds a violin makes! Depressing music, I say. Parsons are for preaching to saints, encouraging the mossbacks, and fellowshipping with the youth. As I recall, all you were asked to do was visit each of us regularly. Whoever told you we wanted you to saw out sordid notes on a violin?"

"The informer."

"The informer? Who is the informer?"

"Whoever he is, he knows every move I make. But, oh, Miss Hawksbury, I really must go at once." One foot moved uneasily forward as if it would like to get away sooner than the rest of him. "I shall be a minute and a half late as it is." He ran from the yard with the sounds of the dog yipping in the background.

Maybelle was standing on the porch, arms akimbo, waiting for him. She looked none too happy. "You are late, Brother Harry," she scolded, "and this is no way to start a series of important lessons."

"I—well, I went by to excuse myself from my visit with Miss Hawksbury."

"You should have excused yourself more expediently."

"She said—she said parsons were not expected to be musicians, too."

"Fiona Hawksbury's brain is as empty as a loft in a

seven-year drought. I don't care what she told you; she has no spiritual insight. She is carnally minded and wouldn't know a revelation if it fell on her head. The Lord revealed to me that you would be a great musician. A virtuoso."

"A—what?"

"A genius with the bow. Bring your violin in, and we will get started."

In the parlor, Harry unsnapped the case and lifted the violin out. "Is it in tune?" Maybelle asked.

"I don't know." He pushed it toward her.

"I will strike the notes on the piano, and you will tune it," she suggested.

"How—?"

"Turn those little pegs. The strings are wrapped around them. Just twist until the string, when plucked, makes the same sound as I make on the piano. It is as simple as that." She thumped on a key.

"No, that's the wrong peg, Brother Harry. The one on the bottom nearest you controls the string we are trying to tune. Not too tight now. You'll break a string." Harry had an urge to twist the peg with all his might and hear the delicious damage.

"There." She stopped him. However, his ears couldn't make the pitch of the string correspond with her note at all. To him it sounded discordant. But she was a musician, and he wasn't.

"Next."

Finally, the four pegs had been turned either one way or the other. "Now the bow," she instructed. "Tighten it. Oh, here, I will do it for you." She worked at the floss until it was taut.

"Now, under your chin goes the instrument, my dear man." She made a clucking noise with her tongue. "Hold the bow lightly with the fingers of the right hand."

Harry obeyed, feeling awkward.

"Now, slide the bow across the strings."

A miserable bawl came from the violin. "Wonderful!" she shouted. "Oh, I knew you had talent! You are getting the hang of it with the first maneuver of the bow. But now it is time for us to take a break. You'll lean back on the sofa, and I will bring you a glass of juice. We'll relax for a few moments."

"I haven't done anything yet."

"Oh, you have! You have! During our breaks, we must clear our minds. Think of something besides the lesson. About your projections for the future, perhaps—"

"All I can think about is the conflicting stories I am getting," blurted Brother Harry, laying aside tact. "The informant says that the majority insist I play the fiddle—"

"It isn't a fiddle; it is a violin."

"And Miss Hawksbury says the majority couldn't give a farthing whether I play or whether I don't!"

"Who is this informant?"

"Someone who keeps sending me letters."

"Well, I would listen to the informant if I were you, Brother Harry. Apparently, they have your best interest at heart, or they wouldn't take the time to write those nice letters. Fiona will destroy you if you allow it. You haven't been here long enough to discover her tactics—" she stopped abruptly. "Let's get back to our business now."

The second phase of the lesson was worse. By way of "instructions," Maybelle put her hand on his to guide it. Then she practically wrapped her arms about him to show the note positions. He could smell her hair, her perfume, and her starched collar. His stomach flipped, and he thought he might gag.

Had the notes come out clearer, he could have taken courage, but they didn't. The same raspy, sawing wail belched forth with each sweep of the bow.

"You are improving, Brother Harry," Maybelle cried, clapping her hands together. "Oh, the mystery of tone! Before long, we will be playing beautiful duets."

Brother Harry could think of nothing that would repulse him more than a concert with Maybelle Davis. In the high court of reason, the whole scheme seemed absurd. What could he do to get out of this predicament? Leave town for a few days?

CHAPTER 12

The Fishing Trip

Brother Harry set aside a Saturday for the fishing trip with the boys who attended his church. Miss Davis had pigeonholed the day for another music lesson, but he balked. He couldn't devote his entire life to the violin, he said. It would do no harm to skip one lesson.

"Oh, Brother Harry! We will surely lose ground," she upbraided. "And you are doing so nicely."

"I have given my word to take the children fishing," he declared. "I shall not disappoint them."

Before Saturday, another letter came to his address. *Your priorities are creeping out of line, Parson,* it said. *You are tottering toward worldly pleasures when you choose a fishing trip over weightier matters. What kind of example are you setting for our youth when you forfeit an opportunity to better your ministry to gallivant to the river? Think on these things.* It had no closing salutation.

Harry gave scant attention to the message. It was important that he take Luther fishing. Luther talked more and more about the hobo. The hobo, he said, had spent several hours in the widow's home playing marbles with the boys on the birthday of the youngest. He had carved a whistle for John-John, and the youngster carried it with him everywhere he went. The hobo seemed to be taking more and more liberties with the family.

Ignoring the protests of Maybelle Davis and the anonymous letters, Brother Harry had continued to take his shirts to the widow. He convinced himself that no one had a right to debate the issue of his laundry, inwardly delighted when the widow refused to turn his shirts to Miss Davis for delivery. The shirts provided his only excuse to see the widow and her children. He wished he had more shirts or more reasons to call.

He and the widow compared gardens when he went for his ironing; she had laughed with him when he told her about the onions amid his vegetables. "It saved me the planting," he said, "and I now have onions to share." His thoughts abode at her doorstep often those days.

On Saturday, an excited parson drove around gathering excited boys, their fishing poles, hooks, bobbers, and rusty cans of worms. The day cooperated with just enough west wind to make the journey pleasant. "Wind from the west, fish bite best," quoted Luther.

"Where did you learn that?" Brother Harry asked.

"From my friend Boze."

"The hobo?"

"Yes, sir. I like him."

"Why didn't you invite him to come along with us?"

"I didn't know if—if you would want him."

"Why not?"

"He's—well, his clothes are raggedy."

"Clothes don't make a person."

"No, but—"

"But what?" prodded Harry, wanting to hear more.

"He is just a hobo, and he only has one eye. He's my best friend, but the other boys might not understand. I wouldn't want them to ridicule him. Anyway, he fishes at Red Deer Creek."

"Have you ever fished with him?"

"No. Maw would rather that I go with you."

"We'll have a good time, Luther."

"Yeah, I guess." Harry could see that Luther's heart was with the hobo. He should have taken more time with the boy before now.

John-John sat beside Harry while Luther stood on the running board. Harry drove slowly. "If anything gets in our way, I'll blow my whistle at it," John offered.

"That's a fine whistle," commented Harry.

"It was my birthday present. It was the only gift I got besides my cake."

"Did Luther get it for you?"

"No. Boze did."

"The hobo?"

"Yes. I am going to keep it forever and ever. And he is going to whittle me out a top to spin, too. I wish he would come every day. You'd like him, sir."

Harry nodded. "I hope so."

At the river, the boys whooped out of the rumble seat, off the fenders and running boards to find a desirable spot to fish. Spiky grass, starred with small flowers, was shrill with the chirping of dozens of grasshoppers, large and active. Hooks were baited and lines tossed as if every minute must be redeemed.

91

John stayed beside Harry, and Harry helped him with his pole. "I haven't fished before," the child said. "You'll have to show me how."

"You'll catch on quickly, John," encouraged Harry. "Fishing comes natural with boys."

The seven-year-old's first fish was a shimmering bluegill. "Wow, oh, wow!" he ejaculated. "Wait until I tell Maw. Can I take it home for Maw to cook?"

"Yes, you can," Harry said, threading the fish on a small cord of rope. "But you will need more than one for a good meal. Let's catch more."

"I hope I catch enough for Boze, too."

By noon, John had caught ten-skillet worthy fish, and he was tired. He ate his sack lunch, then leaned his head against Harry and fell asleep, giving Harry a fatherly feeling. This child squandered no time attaching himself to Harry's heart.

Luther came and sat beside them. "I'm glad John-John is having a good time," he said. He didn't seem to be having much fun himself. "I hope I didn't miss Boze today. He hasn't been by for a while. I worry that something might happen to him."

"Hoboes who like the food at your house always come back," teased Harry.

"But I think, What if something happens to Boze on the train?" Tremors lay in wait in Luther's voice, and he squeezed back tears. "He's—he's the closest thing to a father that I have, you see. Paw went away and didn't come back, and—and I can't stand it if Boze doesn't come back."

Harry swallowed over a knot in his own throat. "Do you want to talk about your daddy? Would it help?"

92

"I was pretty young when he went to the Great War. I wasn't much older than John-John is now. Paw was killed in France, and we think he was buried in Flanders Field. They brought Maw a flag and a gold cross. It may be that memory makes things seem better than what they were, but Maw didn't cry so much when we had Paw. And we hadn't so many things to do without. Paw loved to fish—" he ground his fists into the sockets of his eyes to drive back the tears that threatened "—and when I saw John-John leaned up against you, I thought of me and Paw. Many a time, I fell asleep, and he carried me home in his arms."

He lapsed into a silence so deep that Harry thought he might be napping, too. Abruptly, he took a deep, difficult breath and exploded. "Why is there war, Brother Harry? Why?"

"Where there is no brotherly love, there is war, Luther. It is hard to imagine a nation that thrives on greed and bloodshed. That is not God's plan for mankind, but as long as there is sin in the world, there will be fighting. I'm sorry that your paw was a victim." With one arm around John-John and the other circled about Luther, Harry found himself filled with a fervent hope that the future would bring enough happiness to make up for the boy's grief.

"Paw has been gone for six years now," Luther said. "Six long years. I try to hold to what his face and his smile looked like, but it keeps slipping away. Don't tell Maw I told you, but I think she is kind of getting sweet on Boze. They laugh together a lot, and she gets all blushy when I mention him. Do you think it would be wrong for her to marry a one-eyed hobo, Brother Harry?"

Harry cleared his throat. He would have to watch his words, for he didn't want to hurt Luther by showing any bigotry. "I think—that is, perhaps there will be someone else—"

"I thought maybe-so you could like my maw, but then the town gossip warned you off. Maw said it would never work with all the tongues loose. Anyhow, she doesn't have a chance against all the others. Especially pretty Miss Fiona Hawksbury. Maw got some pretty nasty telephone calls. She got accused of some things she did not do. With the hobo, she wouldn't have to worry about anything like that happening. Nobody wants the hobo but Maw. And me."

An inexplicable dagger of pain stabbed through Harry's heart. Why should it? Grace Allison had the right to like whomever she wished.

"How does John-John and Louisa feel about the hobo?" he asked.

"They like him. Anybody would like him, really. Louisa is getting grown up, and she will be getting a beau before long. So it doesn't matter much to her. She just wants our maw to be happy."

Harry's thoughts ran deep. It looked for all the world like the hobo was beating his time. He'd have to do something about that.

CHAPTER 13

The Warrant

Sheriff McIver studied the description again: medium build, dark complexion, scar on right jaw, right eye lost in a fight, walks with a limp, named Toby.

The dispatch had come through on Thursday morning. An outlaw who escaped the Potter County jail was spotted fleeing east. All law officers in the surrounding areas were alerted to watch for this fugitive. He was dangerous.

Word had already leaked out in his town, and the sheriff's call box was ringing off the wall. Every caller claimed to have seen the man in the past few hours. He must be here.

Miss Hawksbury's call gave the most positive proof. "He came to my house," she screeched. "I set my darling Frazzles on him, and he bit the criminal. My dog is most intelligent. He knows when a man is good and when a man is evil. Why, sheriff, my dog adores the parson. He barks the gladdest welcome when Brother Harry calls. But when that jail breaker came in the yard, Frazzles's hackles went up, and his bark was ferocious! He knew. And he tried to tell me. Oh, poor baby. I should have listened to him and called you right away. But I thought the man was a dirty old hobo from off the train.

"Sheriff, we really must do something about all the hoboes that are infiltrating our little city. Outlaw them. Run them out of town. Who knows what diseases they may bring? They are becoming enemies to our peace of mind."

"When did the incident you mentioned happen, Miss Hawksbury?" asked Mr. McIver, inserting his question in a tiny gap in the verbosity.

"Let's see. I remember it was a Friday, for that's the day I polish my nails and—"

"Last Friday?"

"No. The Friday before that."

"You are sure?"

"I am certain."

"Then it couldn't have been the man in question, Miss Hawksbury. Mr. Toby escaped three days ago, and he had been in Potter County jail for thirty days."

"It has to be the same man," she insisted. "Bad eye, scar, and all. I saw him, and there's no mistake. Well, let's see. Maybe it was the day before yesterday. As busy as I am, all the days run together. Some days seem a week long, and some weeks seem a day long."

"Thank you for your information."

"Is he a violent criminal?"

"He is very dangerous."

"Oh, and to think that he could have harmed my Frazzles—"

"Good day, Miss Hawksbury."

Scarcely had the sheriff dropped the telephone into its

crib before it rang again. It was Maybelle Davis this time.

"A stranger has been coming by my house asking for a handout," she reported. "I had him take a—" she stopped before further incriminating herself. "That is, I gave him a muffin."

"Can you describe him, ma'am?" the sheriff asked.

"Easily. An old battered hat. Shoes too big. Overalls."

"No, no. I didn't mean his attire," Mr. McIver explained patiently. "A body can change clothes. What did the man look like?"

"I couldn't see one of his eyes."

"Why not?"

"Because he had it covered."

"With what?"

"A patch."

"Was his skin light or dark?"

"Medium."

"Any scars?"

"Only one that I could see."

"Where?"

"On his cheek."

"Which cheek?"

"Left."

"You are sure?"

"Yes, sir."

"The escapee has a scar, but it is on the right jaw."

"It may have been the right cheek. Anyhow, it was the opposite side from the bad eye. I didn't pay much attention."

"Thank you, Miss Davis."

Such confusing reports! Miss Hawksbury's time element was off, and Miss Davis's scar and eye report was erroneous.

Others called, but they were sure their sightings were of a hobo and not a murderer. One labeled the man she had encountered a "gentle old fellow who wouldn't harm a flea." Luther Allison called with a worry that the sheriff would confuse the fugitive with a transient whom he claimed as his "best friend."

The sheriff waved Brother Harry to a halt as he drove down Main Street. "The town is in an uproar, reverend," he said. "Have you heard?"

"No, sir," Harry answered.

"That's right. You don't have a telephone," the sheriff recalled. "The problem concerns an escaped convict. A violent man. He reportedly has been seen in our area. The women are terrified and justifiably so. This man might show up at church; sometimes they do."

"How shall I identify him?" asked the parson.

"It shouldn't be hard. He is missing an eye, lost in a fight. The right eye. He has a scar on his chin, right side. According to my dispatch, he fled from Amarillo our direction earlier this week."

"Has he been seen here?"

"Many claim to have come in contact with him."

"He is armed?"

"Yes, sir."

"Thank you for the information, sir. I certainly will help in any way that I can. If he comes to church, I will notify you."

When the sheriff went back to his office, Widow Allison and Luther were sitting there, looking anxious. "Luther and I heard about the outlaw," the widow said, "and we are here to talk with you." Her fingers twisted and twined, never still.

"Yes?"

"A hobo has been coming by our house for several weeks. He is a kind and large-hearted individual—"

"He offered to take me fishing," put in Luther.

"We are sure that he is not the wanted man, but both Luther and I fear that he will be mistaken for the criminal. On paper, the specifics are very much the same. Eye patch. Scar. Limp. We want to ask you to be very careful not to jump to conclusions and get the wrong man. Please don't shoot at anyone until you are sure—"

"With the facts we have, it would be impossible to get the wrong man, Mrs. Allison."

"I'm asking one favor of you, Mr. McIver. When you arrest the man, give me a chance to identify our good hobo before you make any rash moves. Please. He means—a lot to me. And to my family."

"Why, certainly, Mrs. Allison. Unless the man threatens me, I will not take matters into my own hands. He belongs to Potter County, and they wish to bring justice to him. Please rest assured that we will not prosecute an innocent man."

Mr. McIver's town had never been in such pandemonium. Most had seen Boze on numerous occasions. Some claimed that Boze was the outlaw, a hands-down absolute. Others swore that Boze was not the villain but that he was certain to be arrested and accused as such.

Dub McIver, the sheriff's own son, was one of those who was convinced that the president of the Holy Terrors was innocent. But how could he prove it?

CHAPTER 14

Disturbing News

A secret is like a terminal disease, Boze thought. It finally catches up with you. At first it can be covered, but as time passes, more and more subterfuge is needed to keep hidden something that every circumstance seems to be in conspiracy to drag into the open.

A month ago, his camouflage was safe. But it would soon be a lost cause, the secrecy a dying art. He had enjoyed it while it lasted, and he hoped he had accomplished his goals with Dub and the boys. What would Widow Allison do when she found out? And Luther? He felt a thud in his stomach.

It was the club's meeting day, and Boze sat waiting for his gang. The wind eddied through the damp cave to alleviate the afternoon heat. He wished the boys would hurry. He wanted to get through and leave.

Dub showed up first. "Have you heard about the big manhunt, Boze?"

"What manhunt?"

"Paw and everybody in town is after someone who fits

your description. A warrant came through for his arrest."

"Really? What have I done now? Disturbed Fiona Hawksbury's pooch? Dropped Maybelle Davis's letter in a cistern? Or maybe I should ask what you boys have done. I told you not to land me in jail."

"We haven't done anything. The man they are searching for killed somebody. He is a murderer and dangerous. And listen to this: he is almost your twin."

"You don't say! In what way? Dirty socks?"

"He has an eye put out. He has a scar. He has smudgy skin."

"Sounds like me."

"His name is Toby."

Boze didn't bat an eye. "Toby, huh?"

"But he isn't quite like you. His scar is on his right jaw, and your scar is on your left cheek."

"Could have been a mistake in writing it down."

"No way. Paw sent back to Potter County to make sure. His scar is right, yours left."

"That's a relief."

"I've never asked into your background, Boze, because that was against the rules. I trusted you then, and I trust you now. You aren't the outlaw, and you didn't do the crime."

"No, I'm not the outlaw. And I didn't do the crime. I have no criminal record at all. If I did, I wouldn't be worthy to be president of the Holy Terrors, and I wouldn't have accepted the position. My maw brought me up to be honest. I couldn't trouble her grave with a dastardly crime like murder."

"But I am afraid you will be picked up."

"Don't worry your mind about it, Dub. If I do, you can

take over the club in my absence, and I will be back when my name is cleared. At today's meeting, we will appoint you vice-chairman."

Nick and Harlo came along. "Guys, have you heard the buzz in town?"

"Heard all about it," Dub said. "I say they'll try to pin the crime on our president."

"We won't stand for it," Harlo said.

"No, we won't," echoed Nick.

"Thanks for your trust, gentlemen, and I hope that I don't run into any trouble," Boze said. "But what will be, will be. Now, let's get down to business. We're losing time." He made a wry face. "I need to get through here so I can get myself arrested for something I didn't do. Today, we appoint a vice-chairman to keep everything running smoothly. Since Dub is next to me in age, the position naturally goes to him. All in favor say aye."

The appointee was unanimously approved. "And now the dues. I have four bits this week. I did a little work." The contributions put the pot back up to a dollar. "You may need the money to bail me out of prison."

"Don't joke about it, Boze. It isn't funny."

"I'm not joking. And now we are all ready for reports. Let's hear the onion patch story."

Nick lifted his shoulders to his full height of five feet and five inches. "It was the best yet!" he preened. "When Preach saw all those onion plants, I thought his eyes would bug out of his head. He was shocked to his shinbones. 'Why, look here,' says he, 'the angels pulled another trick on me. They planted onions for me. And here amid my good, sweet vegetables.' Then he scratched his head so that it made the dandruff fly. 'Would angels plant onions?' he asked himself. 'Onions are renegade lilies, and angels plant only pure and holy things. It must have been the demons that sowed them for me. Well, I haven't time to pull them up and plant them in proper rows. With my big feet, I would sure as the world trample my good vines under, so we'll just leave them be and let everything get onionated!' That's what he said, letter for letter." It was probably the longest speech Nick had ever made, and the Holy Terrors gave him a round of applause.

"Good job," Boze complimented. "What shall our project be for next week? Shall we give Preach a breather?"

"Never!" said Nick. "He hasn't left town yet, and that bespeaks that our work isn't done yet."

"Have you suggestions?"

"Our games will have to get meaner," Harlo said. "Nothing we have done has shaken Preach; it has only fooled him. I say we've got to get down to the nitty-gritty and do something in connection with his church work."

"We threw eggs at the church before Boze came."

"Whatever we do will have to affect Preach where it hurts. It will have to touch his ministry."

"We could burn his Bible," opined Nick.

"Naw, boys," interrupted Boze. "Let's don't be daft. He would go buy another one, or someone would give him theirs. There are fifty or more people in this town with Bibles, and all Bibles read the same way. Anyhow, burning Bibles is what heathens do, and we aren't heathens."

"But his preaching notes would be gone."

"Some parsons don't use notes. God gives them their messages straight."

"Really?"

"It's true. It happened back in the Dark Ages, and it still happens today."

"Like what?"

"Like God tells them somebody is going to have something bad happen, and it does."

"That's spooky."

"But it happens."

"I got it!" Dub snapped his fingers. "Preach has been taking fiddle lessons from the old maid. He thinks it will make him a better preacher. The whole town knows it. I've been by and heard them learning notes myself.

"Preach is absentminded, and sometimes he leaves his fiddle in his car. We could steal it! That would make him gnash his teeth."

"Perfect!" Boze seconded. "You guys are getting good. Now which of you will volunteer to filch it?"

All three raised their hands.

"I will."

"I will."

"I will."

"Dub sat on the roof and told the gasoline story. Nick climbed a tree and brought us the tale of the onions. It is Harlo's turn. Harlo is hereby commissioned to get the violin and— Wait! Where shall we put it? What shall we do with it? There's no sense in destroying a good musical instrument. What if it is a Stradivarius? There's only a few of them left in the world, and we would be destroying a lost art."

"I could keep it under my bed," offered Harlo.

"I have a better idea," Boze said. "Once when I went to bum food at the widow's, her oldest boy said he would like more than anything to have a fiddle. Why doesn't

Harlo take it to the boy—"

"And sell it to the widow for a real cheap price," finished Harlo.

"And put the money in the treasury," Dub said.

"For my bail," Boze grinned.

"How much?" inquired Harlo.

"Is a dollar too much?" asked Nick.

"If we sell it too cheaply, the widow will smell a mouse," Dub proposed.

"If the widow can afford a dollar, a dollar it will be," Boze agreed. "If she doesn't have a dollar, take what you can get, and be satisfied."

"What if Preach sees it there when he goes calling?" Nick asked.

"All fiddles look alike," Dub said. "He would not know that it was his."

"So it is settled, boys?" Boze hurried to close the meeting. "Harlo will take care of the disposition of Preach's violin?"

Nods.

"And it is agreed that we will put the proceeds from the sale into our treasury?"

More nods.

"Then if there is no more business, we shall have a motion for dismissal. Who moves?"

Nick's native impishness shone in his eyes. "I move," he said, twisting from head to foot.

"Dismissed."

CHAPTER 15

The Letter

It was the postman who brought the letter this time, an official-looking envelope with a Wellington postmark. Brother Harry tore it open with rabid curiosity. He knew no one in Wellington.

Dear Reverend Harry, it began. *Our church has recently lost its beloved pastor. You have been recommended to us as a capable replacement. If you would consider us worthy of your time, please be so kind as to let us know, and we will set up an appointment for you to come to preach for us. We are a group of about sixty God-loving, Bible-believing souls with a nice sandstone church and an adequate house for a family with four to six children. The income varies from ten to twenty-five dollars a week, plus weekly grocery poundings. We will look forward to hearing from you, and we welcome you to join us in a service, whether or not you feel directed to be our pastor.*

Harry sat down, his legs a rubbery substance beneath him. Surely they had the wrong person in mind. He checked the address, but his own name was there: Rev. Harry Porter. How did they find him? How did they know about him? He'd never set a foot in their town.

He ran through a rapid succession of moods—joy, gloom, fear, uncertainty. Then the pain of a man who had missed his fortune by mere minutes settled in. Why couldn't they have called him before he came here? It was a tempting offer, but he couldn't leave Roberts County. Those hoodlums who were determined to run him out of town would think they had succeeded, and they would start on the next pastor. Someone had to stay to break the cycle. No, he could not uproot and take off. But what harm could it do to have a service with the shepherdless group? Any offering they could give him would help, although his motive for going certainly would not be for financial gain.

He realized that he needed a break. He wrote them a short response and asked that they arrange a weekend for his visit.

When Brother Harry mentioned an out-of-town trip to Maybelle Davis, she scheduled extra lessons—one a day—for the next three days. He groaned. *Why must my troubles always come in threes?*

It seemed to Harry that each violin lesson since the onset had grown more disastrous than the one before. Maybelle had insisted that they play a duet, and even to the parson's untrained ears, not a single note matched. If one did, he soliloquized, it would be purely accidental. However, Maybelle lavished praise on their "melody," calling it a mystic concept that inspired an antidote to the stifling air of reality. "I find a release from my restlessness in our music," she prattled.

Whatever her flattery, Harry knew better. He would

never be able to coax music from the instrument. He had suspected as much, but now he knew for sure. Nowhere in his sinews roosted a vein of the talent his grandfather possessed. He didn't want to disappoint his flock, but they would have to take him as a parson instead of a violinist. He tried to convey this to his teacher with no success.

"I'm not cut out to be a musician," he stated flatly.

"Nonsense. I told you, parson, that you would come to this bleak watershed in your musical career. All great players do. In just a few more lessons, those naughty notes will behave themselves, and you will please your parishioners with a most glorious rendition. All will become crystalline clear, and you will wonder that you ever thought of giving up. When you give your concert, the music will take subtle hold of the listeners and make them a living part of a vanished world. And I shall be right there to provide background music, to give you confidence, to ignite you with inspiration!"

He didn't want to be ignited. He never wanted to return for another bothersome lesson. He hated the wasted time, the worthless effort, and his teacher's inflexible will. He could be visiting the widow.

How could he escape without being rude? He was treading on thin ice. If he offended the woman that the whole town had picked for his bride, it might not bode well for him. Why, oh, why did they wish him to marry Maybelle Davis?

By the time he left Maybelle's, he was shaking all over, partly from anger, partly from emotional fatigue. He didn't want to go to the parsonage. He could think of no place to go but to the widow's house. Her imperturbability was legendary.

She sensed his anguish, for she invited him in and insisted that he have a cup of hot tea. He didn't care if the whole town, the whole county, or the whole world talked. Let them say what they would. This was his haven, and here he would stay until his spirit calmed.

Luther came in; his eyes were red from crying. "I can't find him anywhere, Maw," he said. "I'm afraid he is gone."

"Did you lose an animal?" asked the parson.

"No." Fresh tears started. "I've lost my best friend."

"Your best friend?"

"Boze. When the outlaw scare came up, Boze disappeared. I'm sure he didn't want to cause any trouble."

"Brother Harry, do you remember my asking you to see what you could find out about the hobo?" the widow asked.

"I remember."

"What did you learn?"

"Nothing. I met the train several times and talked with a dozen or more boxcar bums, but none knew the man you described. Each promised to watch for him, and each will keep his promise. Hoboes are congenial folk, even though most are rootless."

"This one had stolen our hearts," Mrs. Allison said. "I have never loved anyone since Jonathan's death, but I believe I truly fell in love with Boze. I would have married him if he had asked me." She turned a pretty pink at the confession.

"Sister Allison!" gasped Brother Harry. "You would have married a hobo without knowing his past?"

"Yes," she said. "When it comes to character, I am hard to fool, sir. Money, position, or name matters not to me. It is the man beneath the trappings that matters. And beneath that hobo's frayed outside was a real man inside. I believe he will return to us—to me and the children—someday. In that one eye of his, I saw tender affection for the four of us." She lowered her head. "And especially for me as a woman."

How could the parson say, "For your sake, I hope he will be back," when he wanted more than anything for this lonely widow to favor him? What could he do to win her?

"What—what made you love him so?"

"I didn't have to pretend with Boze," she said. "He accepted me for what I am. He didn't mind if my hair was mussed, my apron stained. Neither was he the ideal of every single woman in town. I had him all to myself. No competition. We had a lot in common, you see. I know the bite of poverty, and I know the sting of loneliness. I am acquainted with hard times."

"I see." Harry did see. "And could you not be the wife of—of—say, a parson?"

"I fear that I would never be accepted. Not here, anyway."

Harry saw that, too. "My purpose for being here is twofold," he said. Whatever his former reticence, he was now past it. "Actually, threefold. First, this is the only place I could think of where I might find a morsel of peace. Second, I've come to tell you that I am considering another pastorate." Until this moment, he didn't know that himself.

"Oh, please, Brother Harry, don't leave us." Tears came to the widow's eyes. "You are the best pastor we have ever had. You are doing more good for our community than you can ever know. Everyone loves you. Why would you leave? Because of the persecution?"

"It has nothing to do with persecution, Sister Allison. To be completely truthful, the young pranksters have done me more good than harm. They put gasoline in my car and planted my onions for me. It's just that—that— my heart—that is, well, it is hard to explain."

"You deserve a better church—and a bigger—"

"No, no! It isn't that." How could he tell her that it was her—her devotion to the hobo that made him want to relocate? How could he say that he wanted to leave Roberts County on her account and make her understand? How could he explain the yearning in his bosom, the feeling of emotions rising in him that filled his thoughts by day and got into his dreams by night?

"But you said you were here for three reasons."

"Yes. The third reason I am here," he said, studying the toes of his lace-up shoes, "is to give Luther my grandfather's violin. I will never be a musician, and I am tired of trying to be someone I am not. Someone might as well have it who can get some benefit from it."

Luther's eyes brimmed with delight. "Oh, Brother Harry! That is so kind of you!" On an impulse, he threw his arms around the parson. "I will thank you forever."

"My grandfather was a great musician. He played for dances until Jesus saved his soul. Then he played for the kingdom. He could play 'Heaven's Golden Gates' and make you see them in your mind. But I didn't inherit that part of him. My fingers are stiff, and my ear dull. I feel awkward trying to hold the bow in position. Music is in one's bones, or it isn't. In mine, it isn't."

"Luther will make you proud of him, Brother Harry," the widow predicted. The soft pronouncement threatened to unhinge Harry. He tried to close his mind to it. "I've wanted him to have a violin since he was six years old but could never afford to buy one."

"Miss Davis will be quite upset with me," he chuckled, "but it really doesn't matter since I probably won't be around to catch her ire."

The widow turned her head away. A perverse little pleasure grabbed Harry at the thought that she did not want him to move away. She did care for him, and she couldn't hide it.

"May I have the violin soon?" Luther was asking.

"Today."

However, when Harry went to his vehicle to get the instrument, it was nowhere to be found.

CHAPTER 16
The Hobo's Absence

Nobody saw the hobo the following week, leaving some to suspect that he, about to be caught, had hopped a freight train and left the country. Sheriff McIver's disappointment was apparent. His name would not command emblazoned headlines for the capture of a notorious character.

Nor was Boze at the Holy Terrors meeting on Friday. Dub conducted the meeting in an official manner.

"This meeting will come to order," he said, "and due to our president's absence, I as vice-chairman will fill his chair. Let's have the dues."

"I brought the dollar from the sale of Preach's violin," Harlo emptied his pocket of dimes, nickels, and pennies.

"Where is Boze?" asked Nick.

"We ask no questions and trust all members," Dub reminded.

"Will he be back?"

"He will be back. Now for the bedtime story. How about the fiddle, Harlo?"

"I followed the parson to his music lesson," Harlo reported. "I hid in the storage building across the street that belongs to the general store. But I could still hear the music. Ouch! It was terrible!"

"We don't care about the history, Harlo," Dub said. "Get on with the report."

"When the parson left for the widow's house, I followed at a safe distance. Then when Preach went inside, I slipped around his car and took the violin. There wasn't a lot of romance to the theft; it was quite simple. Just walked to the car and grabbed the case by its handle.

"And I had no trouble selling it to Luther. I waited while the widow counted out her egg money, and the girl emptied her clay piggy bank. They didn't quibble over the price. They all wanted Luther to have the instrument. And Dub is right. Louisa is a fetching lass."

The look that Dub shot Harlo didn't bypass Nick's attention. "Ha! Jealous, aren't you, Dub?" In Boze's absence, it was Harlo who caught Dub's swinging fist.

"Rules."

At once Dub became all business. "What is our blueprint for the coming week? The subject is open for discussion."

"We need to be putting some real pressure on Preach," suggested Harlo. "He has outstayed his time in Roberts County."

"Yeah," piped Nick. "Last Sunday my aunt went to church. If she gets religion, she won't let me roll tobacco in her house." Nick, orphaned at a young age, lived with his aunt, a clueless woman ill-equipped to cope with a fourteen-year-old delinquent. "And nix on that!"

Dub rubbed his chin. "I've been thinking. I will be nineteen on my next birthday. When we are married and have families of our own, we may need a church and a parson."

"Not I," said Nick. "I'm not ever going to church. It is always, 'You can't do this, and you can't do that, or you'll burn in hell—'"

"But churches have wonderful meals at fifth Sunday dinners," Dub reminded.

"Are you going soft on us, Dub?" Harlo squinted.

"Could be."

"Then you can't be a Holy Terror," stated Nick.

"Okay. What are your plans for toppling Preach this week?" surrendered Dub.

"Let's topple everything in his house," proffered Nick. "Total vandalism."

"With him in it?"

"With him in it or out of it."

"You two are witless," Dub said. "He will report us, and the whole town will be after our hides."

"If he gives us any flack, we'll tie him up hand and hoof and gag him."

"We can't kill him," Dub warned. "We would be charged with murder."

"That's right, Nick," agreed Harlo. "And Boze would be mad because as president of our gang he would go to the gallows with us."

"Preach won't die from a little rag stuffed in his mouth," scoffed Nick. "And he won't starve to death. If he doesn't show up for church, one of his love-ladies will skitter over to see about him. The Hawk or the old maid."

"Or the widow."

"It's two against one, Dub. We ransack Preach's house," said Harlo.

117

"Yep," Nick concurred with Harlo. "Pour out all his food. Slice up his clothes. Hack his furniture. Let fly the feathers in his pillow. All kinds of neat things."

"It is your decision, boys," Dub said. "But we must have an official vote. A black pebble for a yea to the black deed, and a white pebble for no. Go find your pebble."

There were two black rocks and one white. "Boze may not be happy."

"Then he should have been here," Nick pointed out.

"We will meet tonight at nine o'clock," Dub instructed. "I am the leader, so I will go in first to make sure there are no booby traps or loaded guns. Then I will whistle, and you two will join me. Agreed?"

"Agreed."

Dub stayed at the creek long after Nick and Harlo had left. He folded his arms around his chest to cover the hollow inside that hurt and never really stopped. What was happening to him? He wished Boze had been here to handle the meeting. He would have turned it to something fun, something harmless. He would have protected the parson.

There was yet another factor that dogged Dub's mind. He had been thinking more and more about Louisa Allison. What would she think if she knew he was in on this job? All at once, Dub felt very tired and sickened to his soul.

A few minutes before nine, Dub made his way to the parsonage with the intentions of warning the parson of the impending danger. At least, he could "scare" Preach out the back door so that the man would suffer no bodily harm. That's probably what Boze would have done.

There was no one at home. Preach was gone. Dub

whistled for his cohorts, and they scrambled for the front door just as a shot rang out. "Halt!"

The boys stopped, frozen. The sheriff moved toward them. "What are you boys doing here?"

"We—" Nick looked this way and that, spying Sheriff McIver's weapon in the light of the lantern that the lawman held. Nick's body jerked. "Dub!" he bawled. "Dub, help me! Your paw is going to shoot me!"

Dub came to the door and face to face with his father. "What is this all about, Dub?" he demanded, his face stony.

"Paw, we were just going to play a little trick on Preach," Dub groveled. "Nothing serious."

"You and your friends have taken your teasing too far this time, Dub."

"I'm sorry, Paw. Who—who called you?"

"No one called me. We are watching for Toby, the criminal. The preacher is out of town, and I have had someone watching the church and the parsonage lest the outlaw find himself a hideout here in the parson's absence."

"He isn't going to shoot us, Dub?" Nick's voice was watery.

"I am warning you boys to get yourselves home and off the street. If I catch you at any more tricks, I will send you all to jail. That includes you, Dub. It isn't a time for jokes; the town is on edge. Someone will get hurt. Is that clear?"

"Yes, sir."

"Yes, sir."

"Yes, Paw."

CHAPTER 17

Heart Challenges

When Brother Harry left Roberts County for Wellington with a single valise containing his personal effects, he hadn't an inkling of what he was escaping. The three hoodlums had given him less trouble than the three women or the three dollars a week. Why worry about them?

Take, for instance, the theft of his grandfather's violin. The thugs had simply spared him further music lessons with the old maid and her diabolical plans for him. He had come to realize that her infatuation wasn't with his musical ability but with him as a person. The lessons were her ploy to keep him returning regularly and often. He couldn't continue to carry out her plot without an instrument, could he?

He was disappointed that he wasn't able to give Luther the fiddle, but an explanation that his violin was stolen would set better with the community than that he had given it away to avoid future lessons and more contact with Miss Davis. It all worked for the best.

Brother Harry had been driving for at least ten miles under a glowering sky. The air was still, and there was a steady buildup of dark, gloomy cloudbanks to the west. Curls of white vapor seeped from under the hood. The car was overheated.

He pulled to the side of the road and switched off the motor. A great bolt of lightning scribbled its mad calligraphy overhead; then there was a terrific clap of thunder. The map showed a little village not far ahead: Mobeetie. He could get water there if he didn't burn up the engine first. As he studied the atlas, the sky began to empty. There were no separate raindrops. Rather, it seemed that giant cloud buckets had overturned.

Harry jumped out, hurried to the trunk of the vehicle and emptied his toolbox to use as a container. With the water he caught, he cooled the radiator. In five minutes, the deluge had ended. Gratefully, he lowered the top of the roadster and was on his way, driving more slowly.

Wellington lay some sixty miles ahead, sixty miles of saplings and scrub cedar. In many places the hills were denuded, the slopes pocked with rocks. There was beauty mixed with ugliness. At times the road degenerated to potholes and ruts.

Two hours later, he crossed the salt fork of the Red River, no wider than a washtub, and Wellington came into sight. A large town, how different it was from his hamlet of one grocery store, one general store, a saloon, a jailhouse, a small community church, a school, and a gasoline pump! Outwardly, he was perfectly calm, but the quickening of his breath betrayed the tumult within his heart. *I shouldn't have come*, Harry concluded with self-abnegation. *If I cannot pastor a dozen sheep, how can I feed a bigger flock?*

The nearer he approached to Wellington, the more his thoughts churned. Sixty people! What would this massive crowd be like? Would he get stage fright before such an audience? Would he make a fool of himself? How did they hear about him, an obscure country preacher?

His thoughts jumped about like a cricket in hot ashes. Roberts County. Wellington. Roberts County. Wellington. He hoped Sheriff McIver had apprehended Toby, the escaped convict. He could not let himself think of such a man harming . . . Widow Allison.

That brought his musing to the widow and his last visit to her home. She had confessed her love for a hobo, bringing a little inner pang that she would choose a nameless tramp over a parson. But then, in a way, he was proud of her, too, for not judging a man by what he wore or the job he held or his popularity. Would Fiona Hawksbury look an inch past a man's prestige? Not on your life! Would Maybelle Davis marry a man of oblivion? Not unless he played a violin!

But the Widow Allison was different. Renown meant little to her. The pomp of society was to her the hollowest of chimeras. She loved God, her children, and the hobo. Of course, the hobo would return. Love such as the widow had for him always brought a man back. Even the fear of being mistaken for the crook could not keep him away.

Brother Harry was met at the church in Wellington by a group of shouting people bearing a banner that said, "Welcome, Brother Porter." It sounded strange to him, being called Brother Porter. He'd never been addressed by his surname before. That was what his father had been called. They were showing him respect, to be sure, but it made him feel old. *I guess I am old,* he reckoned. *I'm forty-four.*

The chattering group whisked him to a small park in the city, where a grand meal was spread on picnic tables. There were fried chickens, chicken and dumplings, chicken and dressing, and more fried chicken. There were red beans and green beans and corn and hominy. Some potatoes swam in gravy, and others nestled in butter. Every variety of cake and pie that he could imagine invited his sampling. He had never seen nor tasted such a sumptuous feast.

A bedroom had been prepared for him at the church parsonage, which sat hard against the sanctuary. The living quarters overwhelmed him. There were three bedrooms, a kitchen, a parlor, and a built-in bathroom. His mind had not envisioned anything so elaborate. It would be a sin for a single man to usurp all this spaciousness. He had hoped to find a wife, but—

"Have you a need for anything further?" The question pulled him back to the contact he had lost.

"Uh, no, sir, thank you."

The following morning, he preached as he had never preached before. The amens goaded him on, and he scarcely found a quitting place, so anxious were the listeners to hear more. *I will be utterly spoiled when I return to Roberts County,* he told himself. *My ego is overindulged.*

During the afternoon, he was shifted from house to house to meet the parishioners, and each hostess vied for excellence over the last. One repast had hardly ended before he was carted to another. "If I lived here, I would be as heavy as Eli in the Bible," he quipped to an elder after the evening's service.

"*When* you live here," the man said. "You are out-numbered, Parson Porter. There are sixty of us to pray against the one of you!"

There were no widows in the church in his age bracket, no Fionas or old maids. The offering they presented him was $21.37, which they said was about average for a weekend. There were no hoodlums to torment him. This was paradise!

"I will pray about it," promised Harry. "Give me thirty days. But may I ask where you heard about me?"

"You will never guess," the spokesman for the group said. "I recommended you."

"How did you know me? I've never seen you before."

"Oh, yes, you have seen me," laughed the man. "I came through your town and met you by the water tower."

Harry thumbed through his memory for the face. "I don't remember you."

"You wouldn't," he said. "I have changed. When you met me, I was a soot-covered hobo, and you told me of God's love for me. I thought no one loved me. I had been a miserable failure in life, but you gave me hope. I climbed back on the boxcar, but your words and, more impressively, your concern climbed on the train with me. When I got here to Wellington, I left the trains forever. I found a job, this church, and God. Anyone who can convert a wretched hobo is a powerful man of God, and I told this church as much. When our preacher died, I talked you up until the church wanted to meet you.

"I can assure you they haven't been disappointed. You won me to God, and I am determined to win you for my church's pastor."

Harry returned to Roberts County, but a part of him stayed in Wellington. "I am torn betwixt," he sighed. "Wellington is a wondrous opportunity for me to advance my ministry, but how can I leave Roberts County as long as the widow is unmarried? I know now that I love her."

There was a note under his door when he got home. *We do not begrudge you a few hours of rest, Parson. You have been faithful. But now that you have had your leisure, we expect you to put even more time and effort into the developing of your ministry, namely your music. Do not disappoint us.*

He was tired of notes. He was tired of tattletales. He was tired of everything but Widow Allison. He fell across his bed and went to sleep dreading morning, and when he awoke, he knew it would be a bad day.

"I will have it out with Maybelle Davis without delay," he told the deaf walls. "Today I will shuck some of my frustrations."

On this of all mornings, he had to sew on a button. Aware that the problem was too trivial to bring annoyance, he was nonetheless irritated that the button had fallen off at such an inconvenient time. Sewing on buttons always made him yearn for a wife. A wife would watch for loose buttons. He made the same square pattern with the off-color thread, but being beneath his coat, it wouldn't be seen. He feared the time when a button would fall off in a location that would show.

To Maybelle Davis's he went. It was early, and she was not expecting him. Therefore, she was not in her music mode. No high-pitched solo met his ears.

"Oh, my dear Brother Harry," she cooed when she

answered the knock's summons and saw who was there, "you are back! All of us missed you dreadfully in service yesterday. Why, it just wasn't the same! Sister Hattie was ill, and I was asked to play the pump organ. Oh, that you could have been there to hear me! Everyone said I did a marvelous job. They can hardly wait for Sister Hattie to retire so that I can bless them at each service. I can play so much better than she. I play with feeling. And did you have a nice vacation?"

"I did."

"And now you are ready for another lesson. Ah, you are making your church members proud! I've advertised how well you are progressing. I was not anticipating our study at this bright hour, but I shall rearrange my schedule for you and for God. Get your instrument, and come right on in. Today, I will sing as we play."

"I haven't an instrument," he said. "My violin was stolen."

"While you were gone? My dear, dear Brother Harry, how dreadful!"

"It was taken before I left, to be exact. Naturally, that will discontinue my lessons."

"Oh, no, no! I shall teach you harmony on the piano until your violin is recovered. Now, we'll pull up a chair very close—"

"No, thanks."

"But, parson, I wouldn't think of marrying anyone who did not share my interest in music."

"That's good, Miss Davis, for I have no plans of marrying you anyhow."

"Certainly you know that your decision as to who you will wed will affect your pastorate, Brother Harry. The church plans that—" Her face was set in a sullen, narrow frown, almost pouting.

"I care not what the church plans. I have a mind of my own. Good day," he retorted with a generous lack of wisdom. Sprinting away, he told himself that he would have a scalding letter under his door in a few hours, but he didn't care. He might not even decide to read it.

To the widow's house he went next. He had no time to lose. "I have come," he announced, "to ask you to marry me."

"Oh, that is kind of you, to be sure, but the hobo has already asked for my hand in marriage."

"He came back?"

"He wrote me a letter. He promised to come for me. The children are beside themselves with happiness, as am I."

"There is no changing your mind?"

"None at all." She lowered her eyes. "But next best I like you."

Next best. "If I take, ah, another church, I could provide quite well for you and the children. I'll have a big house with a—"

"I have given my heart to Boze, and I will be happy with whatever he can provide, be it a tarpaper shack or a mansion."

Brother Harry extended his hand for a handshake. He clasped her palm, and for the space of two heartbeats, neither of them moved, her eyes caught in his. Abruptly, she removed her hand from his as if the moment had not happened.

"Luther is learning a song on the fiddle to play at my wedding."

"The fiddle?"

"I bought him a fiddle."

"May God bless you, Grace." He had never used her first name before. "You are a good mother, and you will make a good wife." He turned to leave.

"Oh, and your shirts are ready, Brother Harry. I almost forgot."

He paid her double.

CHAPTER 18

Arrested!

Boze sat with his head in his hands. Time was running out for him, but he had to go back one more time. He had to meet with the Holy Terrors, and he had to see the widow, even with the chance of getting himself locked up.

His motives had been noble, but his benevolent plan had backfired. At this moment, he suffered a bout of melancholy. He hadn't accomplished what he had hoped. His association with the gang, a friendship that he trusted would salvage them from ruin by inspiring them to honesty, integrity and good, had availed nothing. He had failed, and now he had painted himself into a corner. The law was after him.

He had no one to blame but himself. Bad decisions echo on. This time, he probably wouldn't get out with his life. The knowledge was so pervasive that it was like a pain; he woke with it, spent the day with it, and slept with it.

As for the widow with whom he had fallen in love, she

need never know, must never know. After his departure, she would hurt for a while if she loved him as dearly as she avowed, but time would heal her heart. She would find someone else to marry, and life would go on.

On Friday, Boze was at Red Deer Creek when the boys arrived. He had the wrenching feeling that this would be his last meeting with them. In his attempt to bear the olive branch, he found that the three had grown dear to him. They would be surprised when the facts came out about him, because all the ingenuity in the world would not hide the truth. Today he felt like the chap in the Bible; the hand of every man was against him. He would soon fall into the rough hands of destiny.

"Howdy, fellows," he greeted as if he had not missed a meeting. "How is it going for you?"

Dub hesitated. "Uh, so-so."

"We didn't have as much fun without you," offered Nick. "We're glad you are back."

"We almost got ourselves into a pack of trouble," confessed Harlo.

"Vice-chairman," Boze looked to Dub for an explanation, "what did you and the boys do?"

"We made plans to vandalize Preach's house," Dub admitted.

"Yup. We were going to slice his clothes, dump his food, scatter his feathers, and smash his dishes," Nick said. "Besides binding and gagging Preach."

"Why didn't you carry through with it?"

"Paw caught us," Dub said. "He was out watching for the outlaw. He gave us a genuine tongue lashing. It is all because that criminal is on the loose. Everybody's nerves are sitting on dynamite."

"Tell me about the violin." Boze circumvented more talk about Toby. "I missed a chapter in our book."

"It was easy as pie to get," Harlo said. "I just caught Preach sparking at the widow's and took it from his Ford. Then I sold it to the widow for her boy the next day. It was as vanilla as that."

"Did you get a whole dollar?"

"For our club, yes."

"And you didn't stay around to see if Preach missed it?"

"Oh, yes. I had hardly got around the corner of the house when he came out looking for it."

"What did he say?"

"He said, 'Now, I never heard of an angel stealing anything, but I could bless this one for walking off with that fiddle. It means I don't have to take lessons from the old maid anymore. Hallelujah! I could cry for joy!' Those were his precise words."

Boze chuckled. "Seems we can't go contrary to Preach any way we try, doesn't it? I'm beginning to think he has somebody working for him."

"I've been thinking the same thing," Dub rejoined. "It's plumb eerie."

"What business have we to attend to?" Boze asked.

"We bungled it pretty badly while you were gone, Boze. We'll leave it up to you this week."

"You'll do anything I suggest?"

"Anything."

"Anything?"

"Promise."

"Cross your heart?"

"Cross my heart," said Dub.

"Cross my heart," repeated Harlo.

"Cross my heart," mimicked Nick. "I got scared when I thought the sheriff was going to shoot."

"I don't believe one of you is big enough to do anything I suggest," Boze tormented.

"We are big enough."

"I want to see if the three of you can take a dare."

"We can take a dare."

"We can take a double dare."

"Dare us."

"Dare us anything."

"You're not going to want to do it."

"The worse it is, the more we prove our worthiness to be Holy Terrors," Harlo boasted. "We're itching to prove our manhood."

"That's right," Dub nodded, trust written on his features.

"The dare, a double dare, is for a week from Sunday. Not this Sunday that is coming up but the one after that. Has everybody got the time down pat?"

"We've got it. Let your plan fly."

"It is for seven o'clock in the evening."

"Seven o'clock," repeated Dub.

"I dare you—all three of you—to walk into Preach's church, sit down, and be gentlemen during the whole service."

"Then what?"

"I will be there to tell you what to do next. Like a riddle, you will have to take one step at a time."

"I've never been to church," Nick said.

"I haven't been since I was five years old," Harlo said.

Dub made no comment.

"You have given your word," reminded Boze. "A man is as good as his word. Who is going to back down on his vow?"

They looked miserable.

"I told you that you wouldn't want to do it."

"You won't play hooky on us, will you, Boze? This isn't some trick to humiliate us, is it?"

"Not at all. If a man can't take his own medicine, he shouldn't ask anyone else to take it for him. You see, I am promised to be there, and I don't want to go there alone. Please don't let me down."

"You aren't getting married, are you, Boze?"

"My secrets are my secrets."

"All right. You are our president, and we won't let you down. We are standing with you, right or wrong."

A solemn bunch, they shook hands and parted ways.

Boze stayed on the creek bank, thinking and napping until the western sky took on a saffron glow streaked with bars of purple cloud. He couldn't afford to be seen in the light of day. A battery of hostile eyes waited in ambush behind every windowpane. One tip and the sheriff would pounce on him like a vulture. He had a morbid dread of the police and of the publicity that would involve any dealings with them. But he had to talk to the widow. He had written her a letter, and she had had time to receive it. He wanted to hear her say it again, "I love you, Boze," before . . .

He waited another hour then slipped into town under the cover of an indigo night, and just as he neared the first dwelling, a hand grabbed him. He was shackled with iron cuffs.

"We got him, gentlemen," Sheriff McIver crowed. "We

got Toby." He lifted the lantern to Boze's face. "Blind eye, scar, . . . Take him to jail. No visitors."

Boze offered no resistance. It wouldn't do any good. He had been afraid it would happen. And it had.

CHAPTER 19

The Phone Call

The harsh jangle of the phone brought the widow from her chair. It was Saturday morning, and the children were still asleep. Grace had just finished reading her Bible, especially impressed with Romans 8:28: *And we know that all things work together for good to them that love God, to them who are the called according to his purpose.*

"Grace!" The excited address belonged to Fiona Hawksbury. Panting noises along the line indicated a bevy of eager listeners. "I have great news! Sheriff McIver caught the murderer. He is in jail. Now we all can relax. Even my Frazzles is less agitated today." It was necessary that the joyful tidings of the divine justice that had overtaken the wicked should be spread abroad.

The morning died in the widow's breast; a mental nausea besieged her. She wrestled with fear, then horror, then panic. There was a hush along the line. "They did? When?"

"Last evening. It is the outlaw, all right. No mistake.

Bad eye. Scar. Limp. It is the same man who came by my house posing as a hobo. I tell you, my dear Frazzles knows human character. I have offered to take him to the jail and let him growl to prove it is the same man that he bit."

"Excuse me, ladies," broke in Maybelle Davis. "I know you two won't mind my joining this conversation since this is of interest to our entire community. I want to tell you that the hobo came to my house several times. He even delivered a note to—" she caught herself. "That is, he ran several small errands for me. He enjoyed my music. I guess I'd better get me a dog to tell me when there is danger, for I certainly sensed none. But they say that's the way it is with the most hardened ones. They can pose as a saint."

"It would be a good idea for you to get a watchdog, Maybelle."

"Well, I'll ring off to let you two talk," the widow offered.

"Oh, no, Grace. It is you that I called," Fiona reminded. "I wanted to ask you some questions. Didn't that hobo stop at your place quite frequently?"

"Yes."

"And did you never suspect anything amiss?"

"Not once."

"You are naive, Grace. Think what he could have done to your children! Why, he could have kidnapped one of them!"

"He would never have harmed my children," defended the widow. "I have never met a finer Christian than he."

"Christian!" hooted Fiona. "My Frazzles knows when he smells a Christian and when he smells a devil. That hobo was a devil!"

"Boze did not commit the crime that is laid to his charge."

"How should you know?"

"I know."

"Grace, why are you trying so hard to defend a convict?"

"He isn't a convict."

"Of course, he is. A convict in a hobo's disguise."

"He did no crime; justice will triumph. He is a prince, and I love him."

Gasps could be heard, but the widow took no heed. She didn't care if the world knew her loyalty to Boze. He was her espoused husband! He was innocent, she knew he was innocent, and God knew he was innocent. "If they take his life for a crime he did not commit, his blood will be on their hands."

"Mrs. Allison! You are not thinking rationally!" Maybelle's voice reproached her.

"Grace, if you cannot curb your runaway emotions for your own sake, you must think of your posterity. Think of Louisa. What precedent are you setting for her? Think of Luther and the influence that a criminal can have on a young and impressionable boy. Think of little John. Do you want him to be a jailbird? Why, you could be considered an accomplice to the man's crime!" Fiona was talking fast, loudly.

"Certainly, you wouldn't consider becoming the wife of an accused man, would you?" flung Maybelle.

"Certainly, I would."

"Maybelle, I think the widow has lost all sense of direction for her life," Fiona said. "We probably should talk to the parson about it."

"Yes. He should know."

"And I thought it was the parson that Grace was trying to woo."

"She is deluded."

"A reprobate."

"Even the parson can't talk me out of what my heart wants," said the widow. "My mind is settled. When the hobo is exonerated, I will marry him."

"He will not be exonerated."

"We shall see. I will testify in his defense."

"Keep your nose out of it, Grace. Listen to reason. You will make yourself and your poor children a laughing-stock before the whole town."

"I will do as my heart dictates."

"Let her have her madness, Fiona," Maybelle sighed. "It will come to nothing, this perverted obsession. The outlaw will be transported back to Amarillo and will be executed. That will end the insane crush. Grace is going through that middle-aged malady and is losing her mind. Some women do. Pity her poor children. I do hope that I am not asked to take one of them."

"Nor I," said Fiona. "Frazzles hates kids. It is a bit of jealousy, I suspect. He wants all my attention. And until I marry the parson and have children of my own, Frazzles shall have my affection."

"I'm marrying the parson, Fiona," Maybelle asserted. "We make glorious music together. But he will not want her children any more than I do—"

The line clicked as the widow hung up, seething. How could she convince the town, the sheriff, or the posse from Potter County that they had the wrong man? Fiona's opinion didn't matter. Maybelle's opinion didn't matter.

But it did matter that the vigilantes had made a terrible mistake.

She sat in despair, her arms folded tightly against her body. A pulse of terror gripped her. She hurt all over with a cold ache. Her senses swam on waves of pain.

Grace Allison had never been to a jailhouse before, but she would go today. Only she could save him.

CHAPTER 20

Escape

The jail was in a mortar building just behind the city hall. Boze's shoulders sagged during the booking procedure and the walk to the cell. As he heard the cold, metallic clang of the iron door he knew it would take a miracle to save him now. More than one innocent man had died for a crime he did not commit.

There was nothing in the cell but a cot and a chamber pot. No pillow. No blanket. No chair. He considered crying, but the hard tears that burned like acid stuck in the back of his throat. All the plans for his future were dashed, forever obliterated. He had no way to fight the charges against him. It was his word against theirs.

In the pocket of his overalls was the top he was whittling for John-John. It was almost complete, and one of Boze's most pleasurable anticipations was seeing the child's brown eyes glow at the sight of the handmade toy. Now, that might never be. He might, anguished thought, never see the child again.

What would the widow think when she heard that he

had been apprehended? A clot of emotion filled him. Would she believe him guilty? Would her heart find that he had been an impostor?

It was near noon. Bottled-up heat, trapped between walls of plaster, burned with merciless severity, accelerating Boze's thirst. The hot air dragged at his lungs as if he were plowing his way through a solid and viscous substance. He supposed the lawmen from Amarillo would be on their way by now to pick him up to take him to his sentencing. Doubtless, he would get the death penalty.

He knew nothing about the murder for which he was convicted. Had he committed the crime, he would be willing to take his punishment. However, it looked as though he would take it anyway.

He heard voices arguing outside. "What risk could it be to let a woman speak to him?"

"No one is to speak to him, ma'am."

"The man needs prayer if he is facing eternity! I want to read a verse of Scripture to him that I found in the Bible this morning. When the sheriff said, 'No visitors,' he meant strangers. You all know me. I have lived here all my life."

"But, ma'am—"

"I am going into the jailhouse, sir. Whether with your permission or without it."

In spilled the widow.

Boze's strained eyes panned across her face, and he saw her wince. "Why have you come?" he asked. "This is no place for a lady."

"I came to tell you that everything is going to be fine, Boze," she said, lifting her shoulders. "God let me know this morning. I am going to talk to the sheriff myself."

"He will not believe you."

"I can try."

"Do you still trust me, my love?"

"I have never doubted you." Her eyes were sparkling clear. "In fact, the last time the parson called, I asked him if he would marry us."

"What did he say?"

"He said he—couldn't."

"He doesn't want you to marry a hobo, does he?"

"That might have something to do with it, but little. He is in love with me himself, and he said he would not be able to read our vows."

"We can get someone else." He dropped his head. "If I live through this trial—"

"I will be there. At your trial, I mean."

"The sentencing won't take place here. It will be in Potter County. It is a long way, and you would have to hire a coach to take you there."

"Matters not. I will get there if it is on the other side of the moon. I will stand by you, with you. I will testify—"

"Spare your efforts, my brave darling. They will not take a love-bitten woman's word for anything."

"Ma'am, your time is up," urged the jailer. "If Mr. McIver catches you here, it is my skin. I will lose my job."

"Go, dear," Boze commanded. A spasm twitched the muscles of his face. "Here is the top for John-John. It isn't finished, but it will spin. Tell him I love him."

"Pray for me, Boze," she said, looking directly into his unpatched eye, "and I will pray for you." Then Grace Allison did the strangest thing. She winked.

What did the widow's wink mean? What was she trying to tell him? Did she know something he didn't?

Boze lay on the cot for the rest of the day, feeling he

had been clubbed but not quite to death. Stabs of old and nameless fears assaulted him. Darkness seeped in. Shadows slanted across the floor from the high, small window. Evening was coming. The dark hours. The alleys of the night.

He supposed he had fallen asleep, for he awoke with a start when someone touched him. It was pitch black, and he couldn't see who was in the cell with him. He bolted upright.

"Who is here?"

"Shh, Boze. It is Dub. Follow me."

"I can't go—"

"Yes, you can. Listen, Boze. There is a lynching mob on the way. They plan to kill you. You've got to run for your life!"

Dub tugged at Boze's hand. "Hurry!"

Boze felt much like the apostle Peter in the Bible, who was freed by an angel. He thought he must be dreaming as they slipped past the sleeping jailer and ran soundlessly into the inky night. At the edge of town, Dub stopped. "I've given you your chance, Boze, because I know you are innocent."

"How did you get me out?" Boze asked.

"I stole Paw's key. But you haven't any time to lose, nor have I. You must cover a lot of territory before daylight, and I have to return this key before Paw finds it missing."

"Thanks, Dub. I am not guilty. I am not Toby."

"I believe you. But don't be careless and get caught again, Boze. Don't try to come back for the Holy Terrors' meeting on Friday. It is too risky. I will handle the meeting. I will keep them from injuring the preacher. I know what you are all about, Boze, and you have the right idea.

Trust me to pick up where you left off."

"See that the Terrors keep their promise to go to church the next Sunday after tomorrow."

"You have my word. We will be there—if I have to drag Nick and Harlo—for whatever reason you wanted us there. We will represent you."

"I will be there."

"No, Boze! Leave the country!"

Boze took off at a lope, and Dub turned toward town. *That Dub has a good heart,* mused Boze. *He will amount to something someday.*

When Boze was sure Dub was out of hearing, he turned toward town himself. Having survived so agonizing an experience, he could survive anything. He needed to converse with the preacher, to make some arrangements. Thus, he headed for the parsonage.

By morning, not only the preacher but also the sheriff and the jailer knew about the jailbreak. *How had the prisoner made his getaway?* the sheriff worried. The cell was tightly locked, and the man gone. He had never had anything like this happen before. It reflected poorly upon his image.

At church, Brother Harry could hardly conduct his services. The congregation's attention span was nil. There were whispers, furtive glances each time the door opened, and frightened children. Harry's attention, though, was centered on the widow Allison. Her face glowed, and the dark glowers of Fiona and Maybelle could not wipe the triumphant smile from her countenance. She truly loved the hobo, the parson concluded.

That night, nerves ticked, doors were locked, windows were fastened, and the populace of Roberts County smothered in the summer heat for fear of the escapee. All except at the parson's house. He wasn't afraid of the hobo. He slept peacefully with the night air flowing over his brow.

That week, Brother Harry scrapped his visitation ritual. He needed time to commune on a higher level. Sleepless, long hours found him pondering his decision about Wellington. His deliberations kept grouping and scattering. He couldn't afford to miss God's plan for him.

He seldom left the parsonage. Fragments of uncertainty floated his way like debris from a shipwreck. He walked a tightrope between doubt and faith. Was it personal ambition that brought visions of stained-glass windows spreading patterns of soft color across mahogany pews? Did big houses and big benefactors sway him? He had always been a man of simple tastes. What was happening to him?

Tuesday afternoon brought a knock to his door. He opened it to a slight commotion and a wave of perfume. Fiona Hawksbury and Maybelle Davis stood there, robed in their mantles of self-importance, and Harry thought the moment humorous as they stared at his shoeless feet in the silence that followed. He made no effort to erase their embarrassment in thus catching him. The time with God had given him revelations about his own strength that he could not have learned any other way. He no longer cared if these two spiteful gossips fell headlong out of their land of dreams.

Harry made no move to invite them in. "Yes?" he said.

Indignation and fury blended on Fiona's flawless brow. "We have come to tell you about the ill-named Grace Allison. She has fallen from grace."

"Wait." He held up his hand. "I don't discuss one saint with another."

"As a member of your church, Grace Allison's sins are certainly your business. You must caution her, for she won't listen to us."

"If it is my business, then why make it yours?"

"We are not making it ours," disclaimed Maybelle. "The town is talking, and the problem involves the church. You are the pastor."

The sun, slanting in from three angles, made little pools of light on the bare-boarded floor of the porch.

"Brother Harry." Fiona scoured him with hard eyes. "You must know that the widow is infatuated with a dirty hobo. She plans to marry a boxcar bum."

Harry's hearty laugh started at the top of his head and worked down gradually with many secondary earthquakes to the tips of his toes. It was a laugh of pure relish, and he could see that it offended the two women who seemed on the verge of tears. They thought he was the last to know anything!

"I'm sorry for laughing, sisters," he apologized with the tail end of the mirth still on his face, "but I have known about this for a long while. Widow Allison confessed to me. Perhaps now that the man has given the law a slip, they will elope."

"She has taken leave of her senses."

"Perhaps so," agreed Brother Harry.

"You must try to reason with her, Brother Harry! It is your God-given duty. You cannot let her self-destruct. She is not only humiliating the members of our church, but her recklessness and lack of propriety is also setting a poor example for her children!"

149

"I offered to marry her," the parson said, watching their shocked expressions, "but she said she preferred the hobo."

"No!"

"I will talk with her again but not until Sunday. I have devoted this entire week to fasting and meditation. I am making no calls."

"Sunday may be too late."

"Then it will save me the trouble," he said and unceremoniously closed the door in their faces.

On Wednesday, word reached Sheriff McIver that Toby was no longer a threat to society. He had been spotted, pursued, and killed in a shootout with the police when he tried to return to Amarillo. Positive identification had been made. The eye patch. The scar. The dusky complexion. An eyewitness to the crime also recognized the malefactor.

At the meeting of the Holy Terrors on Friday, a sad-eyed Dub took charge. "I guess they got our president, guys," he said. "I let him out of jail and sent him on his way, but he was shot. I will have to step into his shoes."

"You still think Boze wasn't guilty?"

"He wasn't guilty."

"Shouldn't we have some sort of rites for him, a funeral or something?" Harlo suggested. "We may have been the only friends he had."

"It might not be a bad idea. He taught us a lot and served us well. It would only be proper to honor his death."

"Was he really an outlaw in disguise?" pressed Nick.

"I don't know. I have been thinking about it a lot since Wednesday," Dub answered thoughtfully. "Boze had a right heart. If he said he didn't kill anyone, then he didn't. If he had a black past, he was changed by the time he got to us. He didn't seem to want us to know who he was or where he came from. He was hiding something, but he wasn't a mean man. He wasn't cruel or evil. In fact, I've never met a better man."

"What could we do for his memory?"

"Sometimes they say, 'Dust to dust and ashes to ashes,' but I don't know what that means," Nick offered.

"We will put up a cross here at Red Deer Creek and write on it: *To a man we want to be like*," Dub said.

"Yes!" saluted Nick.

"Yes!" Harlo saluted too.

"Now that Boze is gone, we don't have to go to Preach's church on Sunday, do we?" Relief rode on Nick's face. "He won't be there to know—"

"Yes, we will go. A promise is a promise, and that was our last promise to him. As a tribute to his memory, we will do as he wished. He taught us that if we don't keep our word, we will prove we are not real men. By doing that, we would undo the creed upon which Boze built the Holy Terrors."

"So it is seven o'clock Sunday evening?"

"And dressed like gentlemen," Dub said.

CHAPTER 21

Holy Angels

Brother Harry was enjoying the onions from his garden and his freedom from violin lessons. He didn't worry about the notes from the "all-seeing eye," the last of which threatened his eviction. His troubles that had come in threes—women, hoodlums, and his salary of three dollars—bothered him no more.

He had prayed. He had fasted. He had decided. He would soon be leaving Roberts County. It would be a bittersweet parting, for he had hoped to outlast the hoodlums. They would think they had succeeded in running him out of town when, in truth, they had helped him to stay this long.

Sunday would be his last service. Roberts County had been his proving ground, his Calvary. He was going to Wellington, where there were sixty wonderful people, a good income, and a large house. It would be a glorious resurrection for him.

No one knew of his decision save the widow. The widow. The woman he loved and would always love. He had not seen her since the outlaw had lost his life in the gun battle. He had purposely evaded her, for if she were grieving for the hobo, he couldn't bear to see her tears of sorrow. It would break his heart.

She once told him that she liked him second best. If he married her now, he would have to play second fiddle to the hobo. Thinking of the analogy, he smiled to himself. He was a miserable fiddle player, first or second.

He planned to tender his resignation on Sunday evening. There would be some surprised people when he made the announcement. Fiona's fret would be for her dog, which would suffer prostration without his beloved parson to yip for. (But his parson would be gleeful at the parting.) Maybelle would bury her long nose in her lawn handkerchief with its tatted edge and would pretend to weep for the loss of such a promising musician and for the fact that she was losing a chance to be an asset to his ministry. The widow would . . . Well, he hoped and prayed that she would be there, along with Louisa, Luther, and John-John, so that he might have a last daydream of how nicely they would all fit into the parsonage at Wellington.

What would become of the Roberts County church when he was gone? He had learned to care for these people in spite of their idiosyncrasies. They would be left shepherdless, and with the reputation the hoodlums had gained for causing trouble, it might be difficult for them to find a parson willing to accommodate them. They hadn't much to offer in the way of life's comforts.

Yet that was God's problem. God had asked him to move to Wellington, so God must take care of the church he was leaving behind.

The hours dragged by, snagging on splinters of memory. When sentiment threatened to overwhelm him, he turned his mind to Wellington. Part of him was already there, yet it wasn't quite enough. The widow was here.

The final service started as usual. Brother Harry was pleased to note that the widow and her children were seated in their regular places, and she didn't have on a black mourning dress. Nor did she seem overly distressed. Harry's mind clawed for the right thing to say, the proper way to break his news.

Then the unthinkable happened. The three hoodlums slipped in the back door and sat themselves quietly on the last row. Every neck in the building craned to see who the visitors might be. All except Widow Allison and her children. She had taught them to be mannerly and not to stare at guests.

"We would like to welcome the fine gentlemen who have come to join us this evening," Brother Harry said. "We hope you will feel right at home here, sirs." He spoke as comfortably as if they had been to every service throughout his pastorate, showing no amazement or alarm.

The young men caused no disturbances. They were polite and attentive. Their conduct, deemed the parson, was more exemplary than those who frequently turned to give them curious gapes.

There was no hellfire preaching that evening. It had its time and its place, but tonight God's love and not His judgment was reaching for three young men. Brother Harry was wise enough to understand this. A holy awe blanketed the audience in its cocoon, excluding no one from its warm embrace.

The hammer for which none was ready fell in the last

stages of the parson's moving sermon. All eyes were riveted upon him, all minds lent to his powerful appeal. The three delinquents were transfixed, not moving a muscle. "And now, dear ones, I must tell you that this is my last service with you."

Stunned silence.

"I have taken a church farther south."

Fiona dabbed at her eyes, and Maybelle looked angry. Deacon Shone made a noise in his nose. The widow showed no emotion at all.

While the state of shock gripped them, he continued. "But I have not finished my message." From behind a curtain that covered the pulpit's cavity, he pulled a sack. "Mr. Boze has left some items behind." The three boys sat forward on the bench.

From the bag, Brother Harry pulled an eye patch, a battered hat, a powdered wig, and a chunk of coal. "Just as our God disguised Himself in human flesh and came to our world to save us, so a man disguised himself as a hobo and came to Roberts County to help three young men find a better way. This man was willing to give his life for them, and he and Jesus loved them and wanted them to be saved. That love was unconditional."

The three teenagers bowed their heads. Boze had been their friend. The parson was right. He loved them. They had loved him.

"You think Boze is dead. Boze is not dead. I am that man who loved you. I am Boze."

Nick looked at Harlo and Harlo looked at Dub as the truth seeped in. Then Dub began to wipe tears from his eyes.

Many and varied were the reactions. Maybelle Davis

turned several shades of red. The "hobo" who had delivered her manipulative notes was none other than the parson himself! He had known the originator of the imprudent messages all along. Shame, the parson decided, is a hard taskmaster. Without taxing the memory, it replays every mistake. It is like a knot inside one's being that grows tighter the more the person tugs at it. Maybelle was tugging at her shame, her neck becoming more purple by the minute.

Fiona's mouth gaped open, unladylike. Her Frazzles had failed to recognize the parson and had attacked him! After all the bragging she had done about the dog's superior intelligence . . . !

Harry tried to watch everyone at once. The one whose attitude mattered the most, the widow, would not look at him. He had the feeling that she was suppressing a laugh.

The service had accomplished its purpose; he had made his confession. He could do no more to win the boys he loved or exonerate the ones who had made fools of themselves. He tried to dismiss the service, but everyone wanted to have their say.

Maybelle was the first to stand to her feet. "I have written many unkind notes to God's servants over the past years," she said. "It will never happen again. I have been properly chastened."

Fiona got up. "My dog, Frazzles, had no discernment at all," she admitted. "He attacked the parson, and I said a few bad words to him myself. Please forgive me, Brother Harry."

Others offered words of appreciation and expressed regret that the parson was leaving. At the last, Dub stood. "Mr. Boze," he said, scattering a titter through the group of believers, "we regret to lose you, but you don't have to worry about what will become of your little flock here. I am young, nineteen today, but I have known all along that God had dubbed me to be a parson. Since I was a child, I have fought that call. The more I fought it, the meaner I became. But tonight I give up to Jesus and His will. God has an apprentice pastor on His hands. I will continue your work here as best I can."

Louisa Allison broke her mother's rule by turning full around to give Dub a most charming smile. Dub gladly returned it.

Nick stood. "I'll stand with Dub, Boze. He's vice-chairman. If he goes with Jesus, I will, too," he said.

Harlo arose. "I won't be left out," he said. "I hope that our club, the Holy Terrors, can be called the Holy Angels from now on, sir."

Harry thought his heart would burst with joy. The holy angels in heaven must be rejoicing over the Holy Angels on earth. It had been worth the hours spent, the imprisonment, the ill treatment. He and God had won!

But he had to speak to the widow. He didn't want to move to Wellington without her and the children. Could she forgive the deception?

After the dismissal, he hurried to her side, hardly knowing whose hands he shook on the way. He knew he would have to look at her, and for a moment, he was afraid. "I hope I haven't hurt you too deeply," he said, yearning for some sign of affection from her.

She lifted her eyes to his, her gaze so steady and so serene that instead of weakness he felt reassurance. Then she winked. "I knew who you were all the time," she grinned. "I have everything packed and ready to move."

"How—?"

"Remember, I did your ironing. There was a telltale feature about the hobo's shirt that gave away your secret. His buttons!"

She reached up and laid a finger on his collar, sending a shiver all the way down his spine. "Nobody sews on buttons like Harry Porter. And that awful taffy-colored thread!"

About the Author

LAJOYCE MARTIN, a minister's wife, has written for Word Aflame Publications for many years with numerous stories and books in print. She is in much demand for speaking at seminars, banquets, and camps. Her writings have touched people young and old alike all over the world.